Too Close To Call

Also By Tessa Bailey

Baiting the Maid of Honor
Unfixable (New Adult)
Protecting What's Theirs (novella)
Staking His Claim
Asking For Trouble
Officer Off Limits
His Risk to Take
Protecting What's His
Owned by Fate
Exposed by Fate
Riskier Business
Risking It All (Crossing the Line 1)
Driven by Fate
Chase Me (Broke & Beautiful 1)
Need Me (Broke & Beautiful 2)
Off Base (novella)
Up in Smoke (Crossing the Line 2)
Make Me (Broke & Beautiful 3)
Crashed Out (Made in Jersey 1)
Boiling Point (Crossing the Line 3)
Rough Rhythm
Thrown Down (Made in Jersey 2)
Raw Redemption (Crossing the Line 4)
Worked Up (Made in Jersey 3)
Wound Tight (Made in Jersey 4)
Too Hot to Handle (Romancing the Clarksons 1)
Too Wild to Tame (Romancing the Clarksons 2)
Too Hard to Forget (Romancing the Clarksons 3)
Too Beautiful to Break (Romancing the Clarksons 4)
Too Close to Call: A Romancing the Clarksons Novella

Too Close To Call

A Romancing the Clarksons Novella

By Tessa Bailey

1001 Dark Nights

EVIL EYE
CONCEPTS

Too Close To Call
A Romancing the Clarksons Novella
By Tessa Bailey

1001 Dark Nights

Copyright 2017 Tessa Bailey
ISBN: 978-1-9459-2043-1

Foreword: Copyright 2014 M. J. Rose

Published by Evil Eye Concepts, Incorporated

Acknowledgments from the Author

Thank you so much to the 1001 Dark Nights team, including Liz Berry, MJ Rose, Jillian Greenfield Stein, and all the wonderful editors and designers. Thank you as well to Madeleine Colavita at Forever Romance, my family (especially my husband who watches the NFL Draft, which inspired this story) and as always, the readers. Love you all.

Sign up for the 1001 Dark Nights Newsletter
and be entered to win a Tiffany Key necklace.

There's a contest every month!

Go to www.1001DarkNights.com to subscribe.

As a bonus, all subscribers will receive a free
1001 Dark Nights story
The First Night
by Lexi Blake & M.J. Rose

One Thousand and One Dark Nights

Once upon a time, in the future…

*I was a student fascinated with stories and learning.
I studied philosophy, poetry, history, the occult, and
the art and science of love and magic. I had a vast
library at my father's home and collected thousands
of volumes of fantastic tales.*

*I learned all about ancient races and bygone
times. About myths and legends and dreams of all
people through the millennium. And the more I read
the stronger my imagination grew until I discovered
that I was able to travel into the stories... to actually
become part of them.*

*I wish I could say that I listened to my teacher
and respected my gift, as I ought to have. If I had, I
would not be telling you this tale now.
But I was foolhardy and confused, showing off
with bravery.*

*One afternoon, curious about the myth of the
Arabian Nights, I traveled back to ancient Persia to
see for myself if it was true that every day Shahryar
(Persian: شهریار, "king") married a new virgin, and then
sent yesterday's wife to be beheaded. It was written
and I had read, that by the time he met Scheherazade,
the vizier's daughter, he'd killed one thousand
women.*

*Something went wrong with my efforts. I arrived
in the midst of the story and somehow exchanged
places with Scheherazade – a phenomena that had
never occurred before and that still to this day, I
cannot explain.*

*Now I am trapped in that ancient past. I have
taken on Scheherazade's life and the only way I can
protect myself and stay alive is to do what she did to
protect herself and stay alive.*

*Every night the King calls for me and listens as I spin tales.
And when the evening ends and dawn breaks, I stop at a
point that leaves him breathless and yearning for more.
And so the King spares my life for one more day, so that
he might hear the rest of my dark tale.*

*As soon as I finish a story... I begin a new
one... like the one that you, dear reader, have before
you now.*

Chapter One

Draft Day was *nothing* like Kyler had pictured.

"With the ninth pick in the 2017 NFL Draft, the Los Angeles Rage select..." Kyler Tate's parents sucked in breaths on either side of him. "Kyler Tate, receiver, University of Cincinnati."

The tense atmosphere inside the event hall exploded with wild cheers, exclamations, and boos. His shoulders were slapped by thousands of hands, kisses landing on his cheeks. Like falling out of a kayak into a rushing current, bashing into rocks on the way toward a waterfall, Kyler stood, put his head down, and proceeded toward the stage. Cell phones rang at every table he passed, terse conversations taking place as the deadline timer for the next announcement started. Players he'd faced on the gridiron sweated in their suits, mothers fussed, water glasses were refilled.

This was it. Years of training, icing down injuries, two-a-day practices, glory, pain, and mental fatigue. All for this moment.

And it was...utterly fucking incomplete.

Before he could reach the stage, panic set in. Set in real good, like claws digging into fertile ground. A moment earlier, everyone in the room had looked familiar, but they were strangers now, spinning in a kaleidoscope. Sweat popped up on his forehead. His shoulder blades tightened, a harsh sound puffed from between his lips. From behind the podium, the announcer gave him a strange look, the Rage jersey lowering in his grip. *Are you okay?*

The man's mouthed words barely penetrated over the sudden rushing stream of images. Of her. Bree Justice.

Since middle school, he'd been imagining this day. Late at night, his head nestled into the pillow of his childhood bedroom, staring up at a poster of T.Y. Hilton on his ceiling, he'd heard the announcer saying his name. But in every single one of his dreams, he'd leaned over to kiss Bree before making his way to the stage.

Bree wasn't there, though. She was a thousand miles away in Indiana, same place she'd been since he left for college. Same place she'd been since breaking up with him the night before he climbed aboard the Cincinnati-bound train and sped off, doubtful he would make it one day without her.

In a way, he hadn't.

A vivid memory swept into the chaos of Kyler's mind. Another time he'd climbed a stage what felt like a million years ago…and he was powerless to do anything but let it play out.

"Bloomfield High! It's the moment we've all been waiting for. Your votes have been counted!" The smiling cheerleader bounced up and down on the stage, a microphone in one hand, two gold sashes dangling in the other. "Your pick for prom queen is…" She squeaked and did a little dance. "My friend and yours, the incredible Hailey Faye! Congratulations, Hailey!" Kyler smiled and pulled Bree tighter against his side. Lord Jesus, he couldn't tear his eyes off her tonight. Any night, really. But in the ice blue dress that brushed her knees, all that curly black hair twisted up into some fancy style, she was even more beautiful than usual. His heart hadn't stopped beating triple time since Bree floated down the stairs, her father watching with hawk eyes as he pinned on the corsage.

In the back of the gymnasium, they were surrounded by a mixture of Kyler's teammates—most of them sneaking sips of vodka from flasks stowed in their jackets—and Bree's Animal Care Club friends. It was an odd mix, to be sure, but ever since Kyler and Bree had gotten together in middle school after being randomly paired for a science class presentation, they'd proceeded as if the eclectic blend was normal. So everyone had followed suit.

Years later, they all traveled in a pack, meeting at Nelson's Diner on Friday nights, sneaking out to the creek that ran through the town woods on summer Saturdays. On a monthly basis, couples were formed or dissolved within the group, but Kyler and Bree stuck together like glue through it all.

Kyler loved Bree. Bree loved Kyler. Nothing would ever change that.

The applause was beginning to die down from the prom queen announcement and Kyler's teammates began nudging him between the shoulder blades, making wise cracks about how pretty he looked, how adorable it was that his tie matched

Bree's dress. He merely shot them the bird. *"Your choice for king should come as no surprise,"* called the cheerleader from the stage, rolling her eyes good-naturedly.

Everyone turned to look at Kyler and he forced himself to smile, nodding politely. Earlier that year, he'd captained the team and led them to the state championships. In a football town like Bloomfield, title winning touchdowns, like the one he'd scored, tended to remain fresh in their minds. News of his full-ride scholarship to the University of Cincinnati had blown through the town like wildfire this week, making it impossible to walk two feet without receiving the kind of effusive praise he'd learned early to be thankful for.

At one time, he might've wished for a football helmet to tug down over his head to escape the scrutiny, but he kept his chin up in the face of the attention now. The people of Bloomfield drove to his games every week, made signs, chanted his name—a fact he still couldn't believe—and he wouldn't hide from that type of kindness.

Bree slipped her hand into Kyler's and went up on her toes, whispering in his ear. *"I'll meet you out back after your dance."*

"You don't want to stick around and see my oversized head in a crown?"

"I'll see you in it later." Her slow wink sent warmth sliding into his belly. *"But everyone is going to stare at me while you're out there, wondering how I feel about you dancing with another girl."* She shivered. *"You know I don't like the attention."*

"I do know that." His mouth started to curve with the secret he was keeping, so he planted a kiss on her forehead to hide it. *"Or maybe I forgot. Again."*

Suspicion snuck into her expression. *"Kyler Joseph Tate—"*

"You know what? I'm not even going to announce his name," said the cheerleader on stage, sending laughter rippling through the crowd of dressed up high school students. *"I'll just say this. It's a well-known fact that Kyler Tate doesn't dance with anyone but Bree Justice. No matter how hard all us ladies have wished he would."* Laughter, sighs, gagging noises, and camera flashes went off around them, but Kyler kept his gaze trained on Bree, his pulse hammering as she tried to hide beneath his arm. *"So we're bucking tradition tonight. Your queen is going to dance with her man. And Kyler is going to dance with his Bree. Everyone clear a path to the dance floor. DJ? Drop that slow jam."*

It took Kyler several gentle tugs to get Bree out on the floor, but when they finally got there, he knew it would be a moment he remembered for the rest of his life.

Because it was the first time he'd seen her heartbroken.

"Son, would you mind getting your ass up on the damn stage?" the announcer said in a gruff whisper, his big hand covering the microphone. "The next team is on the clock and we need to get a picture before their pick is up."

You don't understand. This is all wrong. Dressed in an ironed suit beneath the television camera lights, Kyler had never been more aware that he was being swept along in the current, nowhere to grab hold. Doing his job inside the classroom and out on the field had made it easier to forget the pain. But now? His future had just been sealed. Being only than a few hours' drive from Indiana, his absence from home—from Bree—had always seemed temporary somehow.

Once he left for Los Angeles, it would be permanent.

He would be permanently without Bree.

"I, uh…yeah." Kyler rubbed the heel of his hand against his stuttering heartbeat. "Sorry, sir. It's all happening so fast, is all."

"It's the cameras, right? Get used to them," the announcer said out of the side of his mouth, gripping Kyler's hand in a tight handshake, his lips spreading into a white-toothed smile for the cameras. "Welcome to the pros. Cameras and assholes are going to be in your face everywhere you go, asking you a bunch of questions you don't know how to answer. Good news is, today all you have to do is smile, celebrate, and get laid." He boomed a tight laugh. "Make sure there are no cameras around during that last part."

Kyler forced a pleased expression onto his face, holding up the jersey he'd been handed. "That advice coming from personal experience?"

"Son, I've got three ex-wives in the crowd. What do you think?"

"Right." Kyler spotted his mother crying in the audience, his father looking bemused by the whole proceeding. No Bree, dammit. If she were there, she'd be cracking a joke to make Kyler's father relax while handing his mother tissue, all graceful and easy. Not having her there was wrong. *Everything* was wrong.

White winked in front of his eyes as more cameras went off in a barrage of blinding light. The announcer thought he'd been taken off guard by the chaotic media presence, but he wasn't. No, he'd been expecting the cameras. *Waiting* for them with something akin to helpless loathing. After all, the flashes and scrutiny were a major part of what had cost him Bree.

Perhaps what happened next could be credited to Kyler's competitive spirit, those lenses being his opponent. Or maybe it was the love for his ex-girlfriend that had never dimmed, not one single iota. As Kyler stood there, having his image captured and replicated millions of times across computer, television, and cell phone screens, a sense of determination crept in. Slowly at first. Then it swelled and crowded his insides like rising dough.

He'd won championships. Been named an All-American. Drafted by a professional organization. Dreams and goals being ticked off a list, one by one. But that night in the woods after prom, when Bree had tearfully ripped out his heart, he'd lost the most important battle of his life. He'd been in too much agony and shock to fight hard as he should have. Too resentful. And as a result, none of the glory that had come after losing Bree seemed real. None of it.

Nor would anything that came after.

No way in hell I'm going to Los Angeles without her.

Chapter Two

No rest for the weary.

Bree climbed out of her truck and bent forward to touch her toes, groaning at the pull of muscles in her lower back. Who needed Pilates when she could spend the night tending a dairy cow with an infected hoof? Everything ached, she looked like a dumpster fire, and she only had fifteen minutes to guzzle a gallon of coffee before her next appointment.

Pinning her messy curls on top of her head, she kicked her wellies against the truck tires, hoping to lose some of the caked-on mud. No dice. The nasty brown stuff climbed her weathered jeans and even dotted her T-shirt.

The family business was thriving—which was a *great* thing. But her father's advancing years meant more responsibility for Bree. More all-nighters at local barns without anyone to relieve her. More exhaustion.

Not complaining. Bree straightened her back and marched toward the diner, knowing nobody inside would be surprised or offended by her appearance. No, the diner and a host of familiar voices would wrap around her like a warm hug, same as always. This town ran in Bree's veins and she counted it a blessing that every morning she had the privilege of waking up inside its borders. If she ever found herself daydreaming of what lay beyond, well, she shut it down quick enough.

The people of Bloomfield were farmers, small business owners, construction workers, teachers, all of them working honest jobs. Content with what they had, even if they struggled from time to time.

Bree was no exception.

Night classes had been manageable when her father was able to run the business alone, but since he'd slowed down, the workload had fallen on her shoulders. In the four years since high school, she'd completed her pre-veterinary studies degree while training constantly to follow in her father's footsteps. She'd become a trusted animal care specialist in her own right, but even with tuition saved up, actual veterinary school seemed like a pipe dream.

Someday.

Right now, her most important job was paying the mortgage, making sure the business continued to thrive, and adding to her sister Kira's college fund.

Well worth the sore back and mud-soaked jeans.

As soon as Bree walked into the diner, she knew something was up. For one thing, no one was sitting down. Every patron was on their feet, crowded together on one side of the restaurant, food left untouched on tables.

She wiped her boots on the welcome mat and treaded toward the counter, hopping up on one of the stools. The clock above the grill said she only had ten minutes now to wrangle some coffee, but no one was behind the counter to take her order. A swell of murmurs and laughter went up in the crowd where they stood congregated about twenty feet away.

And that's when she heard his voice.

Kyler Tate.

Bree's heart shot up into her throat, her fingers fluttering there, as if she could reach in and dislodge the obstruction. Oh no. Bad. *Very* bad. Since he'd left for college, she'd managed to avoid him almost every time he'd come home to visit. Apart from a couple quick sightings in the grocery store, she hadn't even *seen* him. No matter that her eyes and chest ached with the need to catch a glimpse of him now, it wasn't happening. Too many memories, feelings. Regrets?

No. She refused to have those.

How had this happened? There was always a buzz in town whenever the star football player descended. How had he snuck in without warning at the tail end of July? Very inconsiderate of him to deprive Bree of her usual method of avoidance. Whenever Bloomfield welcomed him home, she holed up in her house until he had the decency to skedaddle. If she was forced to leave the house while Kyler was in town limits, she sure as hell didn't do it dressed like a drowned rat.

Bree slipped off the stool and crept toward the door, praying none of Kyler's many admirers would turn around. His deep, rich voice drifted across the separation—humble as always—causing a hesitation in her step, but she managed to keep going. Having him so close was doing terrible damage to her insides, tangling them up like gnarled tree roots. A vision caught Bree in the throat, forcing her to gasp for breath.

Kyler, dressed in a tuxedo on that long ago prom night, bow tie loose and hanging down, his face the picture of devastation. *That* man. The one she'd hurt beyond repair.

He was *right there.*

It didn't escape Bree's notice that she was bolting like a coward, same way her mother had done all those years ago, but what choice did she have? Stick around and come face to face with her past? Or live to fight another day? It was a no brainer.

Nearly every day of her life, she walked in and out of Nelson's Diner. Yet somehow she forgot about the gumball machine. Her wellies connected with the red plastic base—hard. It sent a boom through the diner and a reverberation of denial coursing down her spine. "Shit almighty," Bree muttered, squeezing her eyes closed. When she turned toward the gathering of people, every single eye in the joint was on her. "Oh. Hey, y'all."

Sly looks were traded, elbows were shoved not so discreetly into ribs. This was why she didn't leave her house when Kyler came to Bloomfield. Because as much as Bree loved her small town, they were a pain in the rear end when it came to relationships, past and present. Nosy as all get out, every last one of them.

"Funny you should stop in when you did," called one of the waitresses, Sharon, propping hands on hips. "It's like you knew something about something."

"I don't know something about anything," Bree sputtered, backing toward the door. "I was just stopping in to see what pie was on special. And now I know. Peach."

Sharon raised a gray eyebrow, all lazy-like, rolling her neck in the process. "You don't want your usual coffee to go?"

"Just remembered I have some in the truck, thank you."

"How is that?" one of the old timers called. "You've been out on

Gamble's farm all night. Was it them that gave you the coffee?"

"They're decaf drinkers," Sharon supplied. "Did you make the switch?"

"I don't understand the need for specifics." Panic and the urgency to flee gripped Bree when the crowd began parting. Any second now, she would see Kyler. They would make eye contact. Another flash of him on the creek bed, his face stark in the moonlight, made Bree bump back into the door. "You all have a good day now—"

"Bree." Her blood snapped with electricity at the sound of her name, said in that low drawl. Kyler stepped to the forefront of the crowd. The green eyes that still graced her dreams zeroed in, raking over her like they couldn't help it.

Heaven above, four years looked incredible on him. Extra inches had been added *everywhere*. His height. The athletic breadth of his shoulders. The corded biceps that tested the stitching of his T-shirt sleeves. Even his thighs, which were wrapped up in faded denim, were exploding with muscle; thighs she'd spent a good portion of her youth perched on since Kyler never allowed her to sit anywhere but his lap, no matter where they were or whether it was appropriate. "Hello."

"Hello," she whispered. "You're in town."

His slow nod was so familiar a ripple moved through her. "Here for the week. Can I get you that coffee?"

"No." She flushed over her own abruptness. "I meant to say, I can't stay. I'm going to be late for an appointment."

"Fine. I'll walk you out."

His expression *dared* her to say no. Challenged her. And for the first time since Kyler left, sexual awareness danced in her middle, sending a swift tremble down the length of her legs. Because her body hadn't forgotten what often lay on the other side of those challenges. "Fine," she breathed. "Suit yourself."

For all his sexual energy, Kyler was a gentleman, straight down to the soles of his feet. So Bree wasn't one bit surprised when his long gait ate up the distance between them. He reached over her head to push open the glass door, sending his scent crashing into her senses, the combination so familiar, Bree's nipples tightened until she winced. Grassy fields and Nautica Blue aftershave.

Their gazes clashed, but Bree couldn't decide if he'd worn the scent on purpose. His steady eyes gave nothing away. Before *hers* could betray her curiosity, Bree turned and passed through the door Kyler held open. And hell if it wasn't the longest walk in history, his presence behind her looming larger than a mountain. Every eyeball in the diner was sure to be on them and the attention made Bree twitchy, her fingers yanking on the strings of her hoodie.

She needed to get this reunion over with as soon as possible. Being around Kyler would only make her wonder what might have been. That kind of thinking was pointless. Destructive. Wanting more than a comfortable life is why her mother had walked out a decade earlier, leaving Bree to run the household. To care for her younger sister and heartbroken father. Bree took pride in those responsibilities now. They were what life had handed her and she would be *content*.

Back in high school, the writing had been on the wall when it came to Kyler. Everyone knew he'd been destined for greatness. That he would shake off Bloomfield and put his name in the history books. She'd been selfish to stay with him for so long, absorbing his love and attention, all the while knowing she'd wave good-bye to him someday. The decision was a painful one, but it had been made and now she would stick to it.

Bree gripped the truck's door handle and sent a casual smile over her shoulder. "Thanks for seeing me to my vehicle. You've earned your Boy Scout badge."

Kyler kept walking until Bree couldn't open the truck door without hitting him. Which meant he was close. Close enough to make her nerve endings sing in falsetto. "I think you'd need to be a little old lady for me to earn that badge," he drawled.

"Feeling pretty old today," Bree murmured without thinking, glancing down at her muddy clothes.

When she lifted her face again, his easy smile had slipped. "You look tired."

She nudged his shoulder, determined not to acknowledge it was made of stone. "Back in town five minutes and already pouring on the compliments."

"When I don't like something, I say it out loud. You remember that about me, don't you." Not a question. "Bree looking tired is high on the list of things I don't like."

"Good thing it's my business, then." Bree forced a polite smile, mostly for the benefit of their audience. She'd never fooled Kyler with phony smiles a day in her life and wouldn't start today. "Not yours, Ky."

He opened his mouth to argue, but closed it, his throat muscles shifting. "You've got new rain boots. What happened to the ones with the yellow ducks?"

Was he intentionally bombarding her with shared memories? That didn't seem like Kyler's style, but he might as well be shooting blow darts into her chest. "I, um…" She nudged one rubber toe against the other. "I rocked them long as I could. Last time I wore them, my pinkie toe was peeking out."

"See now, I'm sorry I missed that." Inching closer, he shook his head. "Always did think you had the cutest feet."

"When do you leave?" Bree blurted, making him flinch. "I mean, how long are you in town?"

He stared at a spot in the distance. "Week or so. Need to report for training camp out in California in August."

"Yes. Training camp." More polite smiling. She even gave a little pageant wave at the gawking row of town people staring at them through the windows. "Well. A week is a nice visit. Not too short. Not too long."

"I aim to take you out for dinner while I'm here."

"Pardon?" Bree snapped straight, her pulse flashing like erratic lightning. "What for?"

"What for." His eyelids dropped, then lifted to reveal…nothing. A wall. "Just two friends catching up is all, Bree. We don't need to play this game."

"Game?"

"Yeah. The one where I come home and you burrow into the ground like a gopher."

"Oh, fine. Now I'm tired looking *and* a gopher."

"Don't deflect."

"Oh, fine. Now I'm a tired, deflecting goph—"

"Bree Caroline Justice," Kyler warned, using her full name, same way he always used to when his temper got riled. "We're going out for a meal, you and I. This nonsense has gone on way too long. You broke my heart. I went away and healed it up. Now we're going to be friends."

The air left her, her organs trembling. "You just put it right out there."

"Somebody had to." His voice had softened, but that wall he'd built behind his eyes was still standing. "You have plans tonight?"

"Besides washing my hair?" They traded a quick smirk. "I'm chaperoning the church youth group dance. For Kira. She's going to be a senior in the fall."

"Shit, that went fast." His lips lifted in a fond smile, calling to mind how much Kyler used to spoil her little sister, bringing her flowers to ease the sting of being left at home while he took out Bree. "Is she the hell raiser we suspected she'd be?"

"Yes." Bree wrinkled her nose. "She's got boys on the brain and goes through them like a chain smoker does cigarettes. Hence me volunteering to keep an eye on the dance tonight. Told Kira if I didn't see daylight between her and her dance partner, I'd break out *my* moves."

"That sounds less like a threat and more like a promise." For just a split second, his wall lowered itself. "You never could sit still for long when music was playing."

"Only because you didn't let me."

"True enough." He propped a hand beside her on the truck, his scrutiny thickening. "Now that you sit still instead of dancing, are you happier?"

Dammit, she hesitated. "Yes."

"That so."

Feeling exposed, as if she'd suddenly been robbed of four years' worth of maturing and moving on, Bree took advantage of Kyler being distracted. She curled her fingers around the door handle, opened it, and hefted herself into the truck. "Maybe I grew up," she mumbled. "I'll see you, Ky."

When she pulled out of the parking lot moments later, Kyler was watching her in the rearview, fingers hooked in his belt loops, eyes narrowed.

For now, she'd escaped without making that dinner date. But she didn't have a doubt in her mind Kyler wouldn't give up after only one attempt.

Chapter Three

Kyler pulled his truck into the church parking lot and turned up the air conditioner, reckoning he should sneak in once the dance was already in full swing. Wouldn't want to give a certain someone another chance to pull a Houdini, now would he?

By a certain someone, he meant the beautiful, skittish animal lover who'd evaded him this afternoon. Not before they'd traded words, though. Memories. He thought he'd missed Bree for ten thousand reasons, but after seeing her again today, that number seemed like an underestimation. No one spoke, moved, smiled, smelled like her. Each of her little qualities had remained buried beneath his skin. And today his need for all those unique parts of Bree had swelled to the surface, just having her close.

Lord. His muscles were still in knots. Not getting right up into Bree's space and stating his intentions to win her back had been the hardest challenge of his life. He'd had no choice, though, had he?

Here was the thing. Bree Justice hated surprises.

Sophomore year of high school, Kyler had organized their classmates into singing happy birthday to Bree on her sixteenth birthday when she walked into the cafeteria. They'd taken it to the next level by serenading her on tabletops and throwing makeshift confetti fashioned out of notebook paper.

She'd promptly dropped her tray and gone to hide in the ladies' bathroom.

One would think Kyler had learned from that first incident, but no. Later that year, he'd asked her to homecoming during halftime of a game, climbing into the stands and getting down on one knee, still decked out in his football gear.

See, while Bree hated public interest, Kyler *loved* it when Bree was the main attraction. Even when she tried and failed to give him the silent treatment afterward, Kyler felt it was worth the advantage of making sure everyone knew she was special. And *his*.

In high school, riling Bree up and coaxing her away from her anger had been fun. Like flirting. Later on…foreplay. Yeah, they'd been real big on foreplay.

Kyler dropped his head back against the driver's seat and groaned, memories of Bree flooding in from all sides. Grappling hands, straining thighs, and gritted teeth. Challenging each other was their national pastime and they'd never missed an opportunity, whether it was over chess, getting the highest grade on a test…or seeing who could go the longest without a kiss.

Her competitive nature, coupled with the way she always seemed to slide from his grip *right* when he got comfortable, had always been an aphrodisiac to the athlete inside of him. A call to battle. Well, not a damn thing had changed in that regard. Just like when they were teenagers, Kyler was restless and heart-heavy and yes, horny beyond belief, thanks to having Bree mere inches away that afternoon.

The younger man he'd once been wouldn't have wasted a single second pretending to want only friendship from Bree. He'd have cut right to the chase, explaining he wouldn't go to Los Angeles without her. Would. *Not*.

But they weren't in high school now. Futures were on the line. The happiness he'd been attempting since leaving for college was all a sham without her beside him. So he would finally take what he knew about the love of his life…and apply it. Going against his very nature, Kyler would play the long game. One foot in front of the other, nice and easy. Right now, Bree was spooked simply having him in Bloomfield. If he came on too strong, she'd go hide in the ladies' bathroom—and he'd have a much more complicated obstacle course to complete.

Some surprises were in order, however, or Kyler would never get his chance to win back Bree. Which meant he'd be chaperoning a church dance tonight.

Kyler shut off the ignition and climbed out of his truck, snatching up the bouquet of sunflowers he'd bought at the last minute. Striding up the cobblestone walkway, he marveled over how the church seemed to shrink a little more every time he came home for a visit from Cincinnati. Music drifted on the summer wind as he skirted around back to the rear entrance. A minute later, he walked into the gym. It looked half the size of the one in his memory, but he still had to pause in the doorway, held there by the rush of the past.

Refreshment table to the right. Bleachers to the left. Dancing in the middle. DJ booth in the corner. Nothing had changed except the faces.

Through the darkness, there was one feminine figure sitting in the bleachers he would recognize ten lifetimes from now, her right leg jiggling to the beat. Seeing Bree with her hair loose, an amused smile on her face, Kyler's arm lost power, the bouquet slapping down against his thigh. As if she'd heard the smack of paper on denim, Bree's head turned, back straightening.

Good thing he stood between her and the exit.

Holding up his free hand in a conciliatory gesture, Kyler approached Bree where she sat quivering in the bleachers. In his wake, exclamations went off like little explosions; eyes bugged out. Kids stopped dancing. It was unfortunate he couldn't walk into a room in Bloomfield without making a scene, but he'd learned that if he acted casual, most people would follow suit. And keeping his focus locked on Bree wasn't difficult. Not in the least. Not when she was wearing a white summer dress. Not when he could remember her sitting in those same bleachers years earlier, tucked into his side.

"Evening, Bree."

"Ky," she returned with a suspicious look. "This sure is a coincidence."

"Isn't it?" Keeping his features schooled, he tipped his head in the direction of the dance floor. "My cousin's wife's nephew is out there. When I heard he'd be in attendance, I just had to volunteer my services, same as you. Keeping the next generation honest is a team effort."

"Uh-huh." Humor sparked in her eyes. "How many cousins did you call before finding a connection?"

"Just one." Her skeptical eyebrow lift made his lips twitch. "It's more of a phone tree situation."

"Is it now?" She sized him up with a glance. "First night in town and you're skipping out on your mama's dinner. She can't be happy about it."

He conceded her point with a nod. "You reckon I should save these flowers for her?"

"If you brought them for me?" Her chin lifted, hands folding over one knee. "Yes, give them to Mama instead."

"They're for your sister."

As he'd known it would, the fight fled her in a giant wave. Tension deserted every line of her sexy body, leaving her pliant against the bleacher step behind her. A visual reminder of how Kyler used to rob her of tension in a very different way. *God,* she looked hot. Even while pouting. "Aw, why'd you have to go and do that?"

Kyler sat down on the creaky wooden step beside her. "You're glad I did."

"I know. You don't have to point it out." Chewing her lip, she cut a glance at the dance floor. "I was sitting here trying to decide something."

"Lay it on me, supergirl."

Her lips parted at the nickname he'd bestowed on her years ago. After her mother left, Bree had assumed so much responsibility, playing mom to Kira, helping her father run the family business and never once letting her grades suffer. The first time he'd called her supergirl, she'd sobbed for an hour in his arms, showing Kyler how much the added responsibility had taken a toll. How hard it had been to face every day, no matter how difficult. Afterward, she'd tearfully asked him if he still thought the nickname fit. *Fits even better now,* he'd said.

It took Bree a few seconds to continue, but she didn't ask Kyler not to call her supergirl anymore. So he considered it a victory. "Kira's *date* didn't bring her flowers tonight. Didn't even come to the door. Have boys changed so much in four years or…" Something seemed to dawn on her. "You know what? Never mind."

A laugh worked its way up from Kyler's chest. "You were asking yourself if boys have changed or if they were always useless. And maybe I just happened to be the exception."

"That's *not* what I was going to say." The metal was back in her spine, lips pursed together in a way that drove him crazy. "Actually, I was wondering if being a big college star would give you an ego. You just answered my question."

"Liar." He winked to soften the accusation. "And *you* were the exception. Not the other way around. That's why I brought flowers and shook your daddy's hand at the door. I knew there'd never be another Bree Justice."

Damn. Now maybe he shouldn't have said that, seeing as how his strategy was to play the long game. He'd never been much good at keeping the truth to himself, though. Bree stared over at him from beneath her eyelashes, that pulse he used to kiss every chance he got fluttering at the base on her neck. "W-well, maybe there were no other *Brees*." She nudged him with her elbow, but the effort was half-hearted at best. "But I bet there's been gaggles of Mindys and Beckys and Crystals over the last four years, am I right?"

His throat ached with the sudden need to shout. If she only knew how *wrong* she was. When he'd first arrived in Cincinnati, he'd been so damn angry and hurt that he'd wanted to accept every single proposition that came his way. Women flocked to college football players like bees to honey—and once he'd been named an All-American, the whispered invitations had been inescapable. Constant and blatant. A few times, he'd even gotten as far as saying yes. Right before growing sick to his stomach and canceling at the last minute.

Truth was, he hadn't been with a woman since prom night with Bree.

The night she'd shattered him.

If he told her the truth now, there would be no chance of getting those broken pieces back together, though. Best to evade and clear up any misunderstandings later.

"Sure, you know how it is," Kyler managed around the golf ball in his throat. "No one special, though."

Her expression didn't change. If possible, it turned to stone. But when she went back to observing the dance floor, Kyler saw that her fingers were clutched together in her lap. "Yeah, I know how it is."

Wrong. It didn't matter *how it is* or how the athlete-groupie lifestyle operated. It didn't operate *him*. And if there was a hope in hell of him convincing Bree to build a future with a professional football player, she needed to have no doubt about that. About him.

And he would convince her. He *would*. But now was not the time to freak her out.

Stay the course, Tate.

"What about you?" He already knew the answer—he grilled his mother about Bree during their weekly phone calls—so he forced himself to relax. "Anyone…special?"

"Not yet. I've been so busy." Her voice sounded unnatural and his heart lurched in response. "I-I mean, there is one guy—"

"Come again?"

It occurred to Kyler in a blinding flash that his mother might have been trying to guard his feelings by assuring him every week that Bree remained single. And good God almighty, the very possibility gave him the urge to throw up. Then maybe go for a casual rampage through Bloomfield, overturning cars and uprooting trees.

Totally normal, right?

"I don't get calls out in Hashtown very often, but their local vet fell ill a few months back, so I traveled out that way. A sick mare. Beautiful creature." She rubbed her palms against her knees, her voice back to normal, totally oblivious to Kyler's mounting agony. "The farm's horse trainer hung out while I worked. He's the one who asked me out, but I said no. I flat out didn't have time. But he must have convinced his boss I was the better doctor because I get called out there for all manner of animal injuries and sicknesses now."

"And this fella keeps asking you out."

"Right."

"But you've been saying no."

"That's the gist of it."

Feeling like he'd been doused in gasoline and lit on fire, Kyler shot to his feet. "I don't like it, Bree Caroline."

Bree rose slowly and crossed her arms. "Don't you dare use my middle name, Kyler Joseph Tate."

"Kyler Tate! Is that you?"

They both turned thunderous stares on the interrupter.

Clearly undeterred, Kira Justice launched herself into Kyler's arms anyway.

Chapter Four

Bree wasn't prepared for seeing her little sister hugging Kyler.

In those early days, when Kyler had just left for Cincinnati, Bree lived with tunnel vision. Getting from one day to the next without a crying jag, throwing herself into learning her father's trade so she couldn't revel in missing him. On more than one occasion, being without him had gotten so unbearable, she'd considered boarding a train to the university to go get him back. Only the staunch belief she was doing the right thing for her family kept Bree putting one foot in front of the other.

For all the time and effort she put into supporting her family, however, she hadn't taken the time to consider how her sister had been impacted by the sudden lack of Kyler's presence in their lives. Clearly, Bree hadn't been the only one missing the star receiver after he left for college. No, it appeared Kira was still feeling the giant hole he'd left behind. Bree wasn't, though. Not after four years.

Certainly not.

Bree swallowed the bitterness on her tongue and focused on her sister and Kyler. It was a well-known fact that teenagers could be irreverent jerks on occasion, and Kira was smack dab in the midst of the classic know-it-all phase. When her face wasn't buried in her iPhone, it was complaining, being critical, and rolling her eyes. In between, though, the amazing woman Kira would be someday soon shone through the cracks. Just like Bree, Kira was a wizard in the classroom. Ambitious. Unlike her big sister, however, Kira loved the spotlight.

She certainly had it now. The dance had ground to a halt, and phones were up and filming the reunion. But for once, Bree's little sister seemed completely unaware of the envious attention she'd drawn. No, every ounce of her focus was fastened on Kyler. Tears made her eyes shine, one rolling free when Kyler whirled her in a circle.

"I thought it was just a rumor you were in town," Kira said, swiping away her running mascara. "And I told everyone it wasn't true. If you were in Bloomfield, my sister would be finding reasons to stay home."

Heat blasted Bree's face, but because avoidance was her best friend, she feigned deafness, picking at an imaginary thread on her dress. More cameras were being lifted, the pinhole sized lights sending Bree stepping back, out of the frames.

Kyler caught the move and frowned, but thankfully didn't join her sister in humiliating her. "How've you been, sweetheart? You been staying out of trouble?"

"Most of the time." Kira gave an exaggerated flutter of her eyelashes. "Me and Daddy saw you on the television. Drafted to the NFL. I can't *believe* it." Her eyebrows drew together. "What happened when you were climbing the stage, though? You looked like you'd seen a ghost."

Bree watched curiously as Kyler seemed to search for an answer. She'd thrown herself into work the day of the draft, afraid of what she'd feel seeing Kyler moving on to the next phase of his life. "I'd just realized I'd forgotten to do something important," Kyler said finally, catching her with a look.

"Like calling before showing up?" Bree asked, still picking at that thread. "Pretty bad habit you've picked up."

Kyler let out a big, booming laugh. "Something like that." He put an arm around Kira's shoulder and turned her toward their grinning, fascinated audience. "Which one of these lucky Bloomfield men is your date, huh? Point him out."

Before Kira could finger the accused, Chuck Brady raised his hand from behind a camera phone, flushing to the roots of his faux-hawk. "That'd be me, sir."

Kyler tucked his tongue inside his cheek, stepping back with Kira in tow to size the kid up. "And have you danced with her yet?"

"Not much of a dancer, sir." Another boy standing beside Chuck shouted *it's true,* earning himself a shove. "I'm better on the football field."

Heads were whipping back and forth between Chuck and Kyler. Clearly, that comment had been made in an attempt to impress the town legend. It didn't work. "Is there a rule that says you can't do both?"

Chuck's friend finally got around to pushing him back. "No, sir."

"In fact, I'm not seeing much dancing between dates going on at all," Kyler said. "Boys on one side, girls on the other is what it looks like to me." He sent Bree a slow grin, eliciting dreamy sighs from every female in the gymnasium. "Correct me if I'm wrong, supergirl, but I do believe this calls for a dance off."

Equal parts terror and...exhilaration tumbled in Bree's stomach. Terror because, hello, everyone knew high school students were the scariest individuals alive. Dancing in front of them was the stuff of nightmares. And exhilaration, because, damn, she hadn't felt her blood pumping, hadn't experienced that wicked belly twist since the last time she and Kyler were in that very gymnasium together.

Which sent her spiraling right back into terror because she couldn't deny anymore that a huge, long ignored place inside of her had missed him. No one had ever succeeded in dragging her out of her comfort zone and making her enjoy it. No one but Kyler freaking Tate.

Scariest of all, Kyler always made her wish for...more. The way her mother had done before walking out on them, going in search of that elusive something *else.*

Bree had balked at his final offer to do just that, though, hadn't she? Cincinnati. Beyond. So far away from her comfort zone and those she loved—those who needed her—she never would have had the option of climbing back into it. Their plan had been to apply to the same colleges and attend as a unit.

Only, she'd kept her *real* plan tucked inside until she couldn't anymore.

"You better not be looking over here at me," Bree called, sitting back down and crossing her legs. "I'm happy right here on the bleachers."

"Gentleman, grab your partners. *Politely,*" Kyler instructed, ignoring her. "Oh, we're going to find out who has the best moves. Yes, we are, Bree."

"No, we're not," Bree said. "Not me. No, thank you." She repeated those words right up until a minute later, when Kyler twirled her into his arms on the dance floor, laughing while she groaned. "How do you always manage to make me cave?"

The old disco ball spun above his head, sending little silver spots gliding over his smiling face. "Because deep down you want to."

Their bodies were still a few inches apart, as if they were worried about brushing together and giving off sparks. And they idled there, separated by a few breaths, Kyler's smile dimming from its position above her. Bree swallowed several times but couldn't seem to flush her heart out of her throat. His thumbs rested in the crooks of her elbows, brushing back and forth, making every bit of her skin sit up and give him its undivided attention. Eyes that had been so good-natured and sweet minutes ago were now dark, like rainclouds that absorbed memories instead of moisture. Just waiting to storm.

When a slow song—"Remind Me"—started to pump low and heavy through the crackling speakers, Kyler slipped an arm around the small of her back and tugged Bree close. Fast. As if propelled by a burst of anger. They were suddenly pressed so tightly together she could feel his warm breath at her forehead. The rises and falls of his every hard muscle, of which there were many.

"Whoa there," Bree whispered shakily. "This is a church dance."

Her words seemed to bring him back from whatever land he'd been teleported to. "Right," he rasped. "We're supposed to be setting an example."

"Yes."

"So I should definitely stop thinking about sucking on your lower lip."

Bree's thighs pressed together, her gasping inhale shivering all the way down into her tummy. Lower. "Stop that right now."

His gaze remained zeroed in on her mouth. "Stop thinking about it or saying it out loud?"

"*Both.*" Trying desperately to remain indignant in the face of *that* face—and that drawl, those muscles, his familiar scent—Bree warned him with a look. "You said we were going to be friends. There's nothing the least bit friendly about lip sucking."

"I don't know." He hummed in his throat and tightened his hold around her waist. "Seems like letting me do it would be mighty friendly of you."

Bree tamped down a laugh. "Friendly or stupid?"

"Stupid?" Kyler frowned. "Why?"

"Because we both know where it leads."

Shit almighty. How had it come to this? She was plastered against her ex-boyfriend—whom she'd yet to shake completely. He looked delicious enough to eat, and now they were having a conversation about sex. And—*and*—she was wearing her feel-good dress. The one she wore when her hair was down and everything was shaved and waxed. Had she primped because Kyler was back in town? It was too infuriating to speculate on.

"You're getting pretty worked up down there, supergirl."

Bree sniffed. "I am not."

"Since you're already worked up..." he murmured into her ear, raising goosebumps down the length of her spine. "Tell me exactly where it would lead if I sucked on your lip."

Four years hadn't changed a single thing, had they? If one of them wasn't throwing down a gauntlet, the other picked up the slack, without fail. Case in point, when they'd been paired up for that fateful science presentation in middle school, they'd both been adamant about *their* idea for a subject being the best. So they'd worked on the project separately, hell bent on outdoing one another. Only to walk into class on presentation day and realize they'd written the same speech, almost word for word.

That day, midway through the oral presentation, Kyler had asked Bree out in front of the whole class. She'd stammered a yes. Then they'd promptly begun boasting about who could pick the best location for their date.

"All right, Ky," she purred, trailing a finger down the back of his neck and watching his shit-eating grin vanish. "*If* I let you that close to my mouth...it would end in your truck."

A rumble moved in his chest. "Yeah?"

"Yeah. We'd drive out to the creek, out where no one could hear us, and climb into the back bed. It's so hot out tonight, isn't it?" She tilted her head and allowed the air conditioning to cool her neck while Kyler's eyes devoured the curve of flesh hungrily. "We'd both be a little dewy from wearing clothes in the humidity...but it wouldn't stop us getting sweatier, would it, Ky?"

"No," he groaned. "Nothing ever did."

Bree almost felt guilty when she felt his erection rise to full mast. *Almost.* Because her own arousal overshadowed everything else. Throat dry, limbs restless, a warning siren went off inside her head. They were moving into dangerous territory. How had they gotten there? "Um..." She sucked in a breath and focused on swaying to the music, but her body clamored against his, furious with the lack of friction. The absence of satisfaction. "We'd get sweaty because..."

His hand fisted in the back of her dress. "Tell me, Bree. Tell me how I'd make you sweat."

"Because I'd be starving and you'd have bought me tacos," she blurted. "Spicy ones."

"Damn, you're cruel." He released a pained laugh into her hair, followed by a groan. "You'll pay for that."

"How?"

"For now?" Kyler's eyes were almost black when he pulled back, but his smile was determined. "In the dance off."

"This wasn't it?"

"Nope."

Suspicion fogged on. "Wait a minute. This is how I'm paying *for now*? What happens later?"

Kyler moved in and brushed his lips along her jawline. "Depends on how good of friends we want to be." One hand lifted to squeeze her hip, slow and possessive, that low voice directly against her ear. "Me, Bree? All due respect, I want to be the kind of friend who takes your panties home in his pocket. The kind of friend who sucks your lower lip until your fingers start fumbling with his zipper. You need a friend like that?" His labored breath matched hers. "Because trust me when I say I'll be your best fucking friend."

* * * *

Funny how plans made themselves.

Especially when you were all goal and very little game plan. The shocked expression on Bree's face was well warranted because he'd definitely just implied he'd like to fuck her mercilessly while in Bloomfield.

And yeah, he did. Christ on a pogo stick, if she'd finished that story the correct way—without the surprise taco twist—she'd be in a fireman hold over his shoulder and halfway to his truck. Hell, he'd *lost* himself in that story, seeing, tasting, feeling himself rocking into Bree while his truck creaked beneath them. That white dress would be pulled down to her waist so he could suck her nipples, rucked up around her hips so he could thrust without obstruction.

Easy, man. He was standing in the midst of dozens of high school students daydreaming about finally, *finally*, getting Bree back underneath him... And those thoughts were causing a seriously unfortunate situation in his jeans. As in, he had enough wood to build a log cabin. Not good when everyone in the place was taking pictures of him and whispering. Although he no longer knew if they were whispering because they considered him some kind of celebrity. Or on account of his up close and personal dance with Bree. It was a coin toss.

"Are you two finished *re-u-niting* so we can start this dance off?" Kira asked, stepping between him and Bree. The younger girl's intrusion poured cold water on the fire below, thank God, but when she waved a hand in front of his face, Kyler realized he was still staring hard at his gorgeous ex-girlfriend. At least Bree was staring back just as hard. That had to mean something, right? "Are we doing boys versus girls?"

"Yeah," Kyler answered, clearing the rust from his voice. "Boys under the scoreboard. Girls by the bleachers. Pick your best five." He shot a wink over Kira's head. "As long as one of them is your sister."

Bree, still visibly dumbfounded by his blunt speech, seemed to rouse herself. "You know what?" Her beautiful eyes flashed, speeding his need for her back to the forefront. "It's *on*, Kyler Tate."

Jesus, he loved her. Couldn't she see it? That he would never love another woman as long as they both lived? "Oh, it's on, is it?" He gave a sharp whistle that sent every dude in the gym hustling toward the scoreboard. "We battle last, supergirl. That ought to give you time to prepare."

"Prepare for what? To make you look foolish?" She jerked her thumb in the direction of the bleachers and the girls ran past her, giggling. "But you're doing such a good job of it yourself."

Both sides of the gymnasium weighed in with a simultaneous "*Ohhhh.*"

"You know what? I'm going to let my dancing do the talking." Praying he still remembered how, Kyler moonwalked into the waiting group of guys, who welcomed him with worshipping looks and smacks on the back. "We'll even concede song choice, right, men? Just to show how confident we are."

"Rookie move," Bree mouthed, before turning and jogging for the DJ booth. Kyler watched her go with his heart lodged somewhere behind his jugular. When he'd walked in, Bree had been sitting in the shadows alone and he'd hated it. Hated her being hidden, no one there to point out how amazing she was, just like he'd been unable to stand having her in the background in high school. Now that she was animated, glowing, satisfaction had been breathed into Kyler's veins, so heavy and real, he couldn't move without feeling it. Feeling *her*.

But...she preferred the background. Right? Isn't that why she'd ended their relationship? When he'd been accepted to the university, he'd been so positive she would get the same letter soon enough. They'd filled out those applications together, laying side by side on the floor of his bedroom, laptops open. Looking back now, he remembered Bree being so quiet while they'd written essays and answered questions. Months later, he'd found out why.

So now he was back in Bloomfield, back to his old tricks. He'd been in town less than one day and he'd already caused a scene outside the diner and pushed Bree into a dance off. What if the truth was just too painful for him to accept, even four years later? What if he simply wasn't the kind of man Bree wanted?

All those years ago on prom night, she'd made it clear she'd decided on a quiet life, far away from the noisy crowds that came along with him. Did he have a hope in hell of convincing her otherwise? What if he couldn't?

Bree slipped back to the front of her lady crew, shoulders thrown back in a cocky pose, but her smug expression disappeared when she locked eyes with Kyler. "You okay?"

He nodded once and turned away before Bree could see deeper, the way only she ever could. "All right, men. Which four among you is the bravest?"

One hand went up.

Kyler issued a quick prayer toward the ceiling. "I'm going to pass on some valuable information. You ready?"

"Yes, sir," they all answered, well-mannered country boys to the core.

"Those girls aren't waiting around for you to take initiative. They have a whole bunch of initiative all their own if they want to use it. But they'll appreciate a guy a lot more for trying. And does anyone know what happens when girls appreciate you?"

"Sex?"

"*No.*" His genuine outrage made several of them laugh. "No. Not...well, fine. Yes. But kissing was the answer I was looking for. *Kissing.*" He made eye contact with every single one of them. "Except when it comes to Kira Justice. Leave her be and that's an order." He clapped his hands once. "Now, who's willing to make a fool out of themselves in the name of glory and potential kissing?"

Every single hand went up.

Unfortunately, that's when, "Run the World (Girls)," by Beyoncé crackled through the speakers.

Kyler disguised his curse with a laugh. "No backing out now."

The triumph on Bree's face when he turned back around was worth the awkward dances that followed. Smooth definitely couldn't be used to describe the jolting moves displayed by the men he'd sent into battle, but at least Kyler made good on his promise. The girls were definitely laughing as one by one, the four battles took place in the center of the basketball court, a clear winner each time.

With the song almost over, Bree and Kyler finally got their turn—and of course the fates had them competing in a tie breaker.

For all Bree's unwillingness to be the center of attention, she could move like nobody's business. In the midst of their competition, she'd forgotten all about being shy and Kyler thanked the dear Lord for that fact. The way she swaggered out to meet him at center court was nothing short of a miracle. Those gorgeous, long-legged strides had him growling low in his throat, looking her up and down when she stopped a mere inch away... And without a verbal agreement, they began circling one another, mean mugging the whole time. The laughter from either side was so loud it almost drowned out the music, and neither one of them could help the smiles they were battling.

"Ladies first," he drawled, sweeping his hand out in a wide gesture. "Better make it count."

"Better watch and learn."

She brought the house down. There was no other way to put it. With a cocky grin on her face, she danced circles around him, taunting him and sticking her tongue out behind his back. Kyler was only guessing about that, but the crowd's reaction bolstered his theory. It took every ounce of his willpower not to pull her into a bear hug as she spun past, all graceful limbs and flushed pleasure.

God above, what a woman. The *only* woman.

If he broke during one of their challenges, though, Bree would never let him live it down, which was only one of the reasons he loved her. The need to win never stopped flowing in his blood and Bree's presence fired it up even more. Channeling that desire into football was his usual method of meeting that need, but hell, today it was dancing.

So as soon as it was Kyler's turn, he pulled out all the stops.

He twerked. And he twerked hard.

It was a tie.

Kyler reckoned the outcome of their challenge couldn't have been more perfect because it gave him an excuse to track Bree down as soon as possible to issue another one.

Chapter Five

"What do you mean, you never sent in your applications?" Kyler tugged on his bow tie like it was choking him, eventually throwing it down on the damp earth surrounding the creek. "We did them together. We...Bree, it was hours, just the two of us—"

"That's why I did them. I loved being with you." Tears blurred the sight of him. "The ones I actually sent in were for pre-vet programs closer to home. I can't leave my home. The business. My family."

He stared at Bree like she was speaking in a different language. "But we'd be together." His whisper turned into a shout. "I'm your home."

Bree's heart lurched. "This isn't easy for me. M-my mom—"

"Not easy for you?" He turned and paced away, attacking his hair with agitated fingers. "I'm leaving. I'm leaving and you won't be with me. We'll be apart. That's not how this was supposed to happen."

"It was always going to happen like this." She held tight to the lapels of the jacket he'd draped over her shoulders, positive it was the only thing keeping her glued together. She'd felt that way since earlier, when he'd arranged to have them dance together at prom, her heart twisting at yet another reminder of what she'd soon be giving up. "Right now, we're in this tiny town. But someday, Ky, someday you're going to be too big to fit inside of it anymore. That scares me. I'm scared of where you're headed."

"There's only us, Bree." He shook his head. "The rest is just noise."

As Bree had known it would be, choosing to remain in Bloomfield over going with the boy she loved was excruciating. She had to hold fast, though. Deep in her bones, there was a need to stay rooted. Right where she'd been standing since the walls threatened to crumble around her family once before. Holding them up was her *job. She'd taken on the responsibility and wouldn't shirk that duty. Not now. Not ever. No matter how much it killed her. "I'm happy with what I have. I have to be." She tried to swallow the knife in her throat, but it only dug in deeper. "I'm sorry. I'm staying right here, right where I'm needed."*

"No." He came forward, framing her face in his hands. "No."

"Yes—"

His kiss cut her off and for long moments, all she could do was sink into it. Let it pull her down. Ever since Kyler's star had started to rise, she'd let her reservations get lost in times like these. When she'd put off the inevitable in favor of his touch, his words. Their senior year was all but finished, though, and after dancing with him tonight, seeing their future playing out in his green eyes, she couldn't put it off any more.

Kyler groaned, his strong hands locking their hips together, rolling their lower bodies as he sunk hungry teeth into her bottom lip. God, if she let him pull her down to the soft earth and use their attraction as a bargaining chip, there was every chance he could persuade her from her decision. And she couldn't allow that.

"I'm sorry," Bree whispered, breaking free of his hold. "Good bye, Ky."

She could still feel his touch as she ran away along the creek bed, scalding tears coasting down her cheeks.

Bree's cell phone buzzed in her pocket for the fifth time in a row. Again, she ignored it, focusing instead on the wounded golden retriever she was attending. He lay on a ten-seat kitchen table, surrounded by his family, each of whom whispered comforting words and stroked some section of the nervous dog.

"Now, don't you worry," Bree murmured, smiling at the youngest member of the family, a six-year-old girl. "Bowser is one tough dog. That coyote only got a tiny nibble out of him. He's going to heal up just fine."

The little girl relaxed, smiling into her mother's hip, although she continued to eye the blood-dappled sheet beneath the dog with trepidation. Bree usually preferred to work in private when making house calls, but when it came to beloved family dogs, she made an exception. It was obvious they were providing much needed comfort for Bowser as Bree finished stitching and bandaging the bite mark on the dog's right front leg.

Moments like these, telling people their animal would recover, made the struggle through school worth every penny. Made it worth never feeling fully rested. She took pride in her work and the business her father had built. When her parents had moved to Bloomfield in the eighties and opened the practice, it had taken hard work to get it off the ground. They were not only the new folks in town, they were an interracial couple—her mother white, her father African-American—in a place where that hadn't been considered typical, meaning they'd faced a lot of curiosity and adversity early on.

While her father had worked triple time to prove his skill as a veterinarian, Bree's mother turned restless. Her father had confided in Bree later on that her mother found contentment hard to achieve. Always had. He didn't even fault her for it, which confused Bree to this day. A loving family, a town that had embraced them, a thriving business. What more had she needed?

Calls like this one were a reminder to Bree that she had everything she needed right here in Bloomfield. She had the community's trust, friends, family. Contentment. Her father did the inpatient work at the office so he wouldn't have to travel, which meant Bree rarely had the privilege of working with canines, most of her calls concerning horses and cattle. It was rare that she witnessed the love between family members and their pets up close. Which had to account for the little spark of yearning in her breast, right?

A family of her own was something Bree had stopped dreaming about without even realizing, it seemed. How long had it been since she'd pictured her own children racing around the yard after their puppy? School, work, and running the house had put those dreams on hold, but they were trickling back in now as she watched the father reach over and squeeze the little girl's shoulder.

Heat pressed against the back of Bree's eyelids.

Shit almighty. What was up with her today?

"Almost done here," Bree said. "Bowser is going to need lots of rest. I'm going to leave a prescription for painkillers to crush up in his food. And before I leave, we'll have to put a cone on him so he doesn't ruin his stitches." She smiled at the little girl. "I'm recommending lots of doggie treats for the next week. Doctor's orders."

"I can give him those," whispered the six-year-old.

"Good. I'm counting on you."

Bree cut the final thread and tied it tight before disinfecting the wound once more and wrapping the damaged leg with a bandage.

The cell phone went off in her pocket a sixth time.

Worried Kira needed her for something, Bree peeled off her gloves and excused herself under the guise of retrieving the cone from her truck. As soon as she closed the front door behind her, Bree plucked the phone out of her pocket, refusing to acknowledge the lick of excitement that slid up her spine at the possibility it could be Kyler. When she saw the name Heidi blinking on the screen instead, she flicked away the disappointment and braced herself.

"Hello?"

"Woman, this conversation needs to start with something better than a damn *hell*-o. It deserves a cymbal crash or a British accent. I don't know. But hello ain't cutting it."

Heidi lived for drama. In high school, she'd been the lead in every school play from *Wizard of Oz* to *Cats*. When the stage wasn't an option, she created her own titillating scenarios, playing matchmaker to her friends just so she could sit back and watch the fireworks. Underneath the lip stains and bleached white hair, though, Heidi had an overly-sensitive heart of gold. Which was why Bree considered the town's gym receptionist her best friend, even though they were polar opposites.

"Okay, I'll bite. Why is this conversation going to be so earth-shattering?"

"Oh no. You make me call you thirty-nine times, you're going to wait for the Tootsie Roll center, baby. Keep licking."

Bree snort-laughed. "You called me six times."

"Splitting hairs." Heidi hummed and Bree waited, knowing her friend wouldn't be able to hold out on sharing whatever gossip she was peddling for long. "Heard you danced all your business up on Kyler Tate last night."

Bree's jaw dropped down to her knees. "That better not be why you're calling me, Heidi. It was innocent fun. At a *church* dance."

"You fix those animals up better than you lie. That's what I know."

"Ooh. I'm fixing to *hang up*."

"You will *not*." A phone rang in the background and Heidi gave a long-suffering sigh. "Hold on, I've got another call."

"Don't—"

The line went silent and Bree stomped the remaining distance to her truck, going through the list of suspects of who might have ratted her out. Kira, most likely. Her little sister and Heidi were Facebook friends and Bree was pretty sure they messaged on the regular. After Kyler had walked Bree and a bouquet-toting Kira to the parking lot last night, pressing a polite, if lingering, kiss on Bree's cheek, her sister hadn't let up a single second. Were they back in love? Was Kyler a good kisser?

Hell yes, he was. Not that she'd be sharing that information with Kira or anyone else, for that matter. The man had a method of kissing that Bree always suspected had been specifically designed to turn her wild. At the start, Kyler played aggressor. But as soon as she got good and worked up, he let her take the lead, encouraging her with his hands, his tongue, his husky groans. Basically, he turned himself into her own personal playground.

Heidi's voice popped the daydream bubble over her head. "I'm back."

"Guhh." Bree shook herself free of kissing memories. "I-I don't have long. I'm putting a cone on a golden retriever, then I have another appointment."

"Fine, I'll stop torturing you. But I want the details of this alleged dirty dance with Kyler. *Grown-up* ones."

"Ha! I knew it was Kira who ratted."

Her best friend clucked her tongue. "Speaking of Mr. Tate…"

Bree paused in the act of removing the plastic cone from a supply bag on the passenger seat. Her lack of movement only made her pounding heart more noticeable. Since yesterday, when Kyler announced *pretty as you please* that he intended to take her for dinner, she'd been living on the edge of—what? Anticipation? Fear? Bree only knew her focus had been hijacked along with her common sense. Because some crazy part of her wanted to say yes.

Not that she would. Oh no. That dance with Kyler last night had proven one very troubling fact. She wasn't *quite* over him yet. Not her heart and not her body. Dinner would only make it worse. Make her…less than content.

"What *about* Kyler?" Bree asked, striving for casual.

"He's here in the gym," Heidi answered. "Working out like it's no big thing."

"It's not a big thing," Bree said automatically, already conjuring up an image of him in sweaty shorts. "Right?"

"Tell that to the string of admirers glued to the windows. A bunch of suction-cupped Baby on Board signs. You know the ones?" Heidi's chair creaked in the background. "That's what they look like, drooling over your man like that. Can you believe the nerve?"

"He's...he's not my man."

"So you don't mind if Karen Hawthorne asks him out?"

"What?" Bree's stomach plummeted. "When did Karen Hawthorne come into the picture?"

"Since now." Satisfaction weighed down Heidi's tone over successfully getting Bree's attention. "I can see that hen in the fox house from here. She's parked at the curb, fixing her mascara in the rearview. That's as good as confirmation in my book."

A pressure formed on top of Bree's lungs, pushing down. "So...she should go ahead and ask him." She tried to swallow, but her throat was as dry as the desert. "It's none of my business."

"No, I suppose not." Bree could hear Heidi's manicured fingernails tapping the reception desk. *Clack. Clack. Clack.* "Hell. You can't really blame the woman, can you? Kyler Tate, soon to be professional NFL receiver, rolls up into the local gym looking like something out of *Sports Illustrated*. He runs so fast and so long, he soaks his T-shirt right through with sweat. It's *so wet*, he has to take it off and—"

Bree dropped the cone, straightening in the truck's front seat. "Kyler...it's...he took his shirt off?"

"That's exactly what I said." Smug. Heidi was so smug. "Now, you know I have a man and I do *not* have a wandering eye, but Bree, when an unattached man walks into your town looking so mighty, so heavy with muscle, like he could grind a woman's vagina to *fine powder*, ladies start fixing their mascara. It's just the nature of the beast." She blew out at a breath. "Good thing he ain't your man, huh?"

"Stall her. I'll be there in ten."

"Consider it done."

Chapter Six

Nothing is ever going to be the same, is it?

Kyler hurried through his final repetition of bicep curls and replaced the weight on the rack. The tiny but functional gym was lined with floor-to-ceiling mirrors and every few seconds, a camera phone flash would go off, reflecting back at him. He pretended not to see them, but each one smarted. Home represented a place he could relax. Let his guard down. A place where no one would demand perfection from him. Maybe it couldn't be that way anymore.

He loved the people of Bloomfield. The saying "It takes a village to raise a child" applied directly to his home town. Growing up, he'd been lectured by the local florist about the importance of proper apologies. Been told to tuck in his shirt by every senior in town at least twice. And he'd gone along with the owners of Nelson's Diner to feed the less fortunate every year during the holidays. His greatest life lessons were wrapped up in this place.

But with camera flashes going off and people waiting outside for signatures, he suddenly felt like a stranger to everyone. Even…himself.

Lord, who *was* Kyler Tate anymore? Who would he be in Los Angeles? Would he be able to hold on to himself, his core, if coming home only fed him more of the same lack of reality?

Who was he kidding? The cameras might have bothered him once upon a time, but he'd grown accustomed to them. This was about Bree. Who would *Bree* become if he took her out of this place? Dance floors and halftime surprises were one thing, but if he loved Bree, would he be so intent on taking her to Los Angeles, knowing it could make her unhappy?

"Ky."

He lifted his head and saw Bree in the mirror behind him. On cue, his gut cinched inward, heat rippling outward from his belly. No other woman had ever elicited the smallest percentage of his body's reaction to Bree. Not ever. No one ever would, either, because his heart was connected to every part of him. His heart knew what it wanted and it wouldn't waver.

So he would give Bree a happy life. One way or another. *How* he would do so remained to be seen. He'd come to Bloomfield to convince her that the attention and notoriety wouldn't be so bad. That as long as they were together, the cameras would be irrelevant. At this very moment, he should be making light of their presence, hoping she would follow suit. Instead, he stood there and stared back at her, trying to telegraph every damning thought in his head.

I'm miserable. I hate the cameras because you hate them.

Here was the truth. Hiding from someone you love wasn't an option because all you *really* wanted was them to come find you.

Bree's eyes were soft, her head tilted. Kyler remembered that look from many an occasion. Sympathy shot through with steel. An expression singular to Bree and one an athlete like himself needed to be on the receiving end of frequently. It said "I understand, this sucks, but don't even *think* about wimping out on me."

He wasn't quite ready to put his game face back on, so he looked away. "You here for a workout?"

"It would seem so," Bree murmured, flashes going off behind her. "Hard to concentrate with all that ruckus going on outside, I bet."

"It's fine." Kyler turned, watching her chew that sweet lower lip. "I can go if you want some privacy."

"Since when do you care about that?"

She meant it as a joke, but the gravity of it wrapped around him like a giant squid. His mouth tried to issue a rejoinder, same as always, but it got stuck. Since when, indeed? Countless times since middle school, he'd dragged her into center stage, against her will. Now he was back trying to do it again.

"I..." Regret shone in Bree's eyes as she shifted. Kyler immediately surged forward to reassure her, but she danced out of his reach. "I have a better idea than you leaving. You see, Heidi knows how to sit and look pretty—"

"*I heard that!*"

Bree winced at her friend's distant shout but didn't halt her progress toward the windows. "She means well, that *sweet baby angel* Heidi, but if she'd only known about these..." Bree tugged on a cord and a blackout shade dropped down, covering one of the windows. "You might have been more comfortable."

One by one, his insanely beautiful ex-girlfriend lowered shades in front of each window, ducking her head to avoid the disappointed frowns from onlookers. Soon enough, the two of them were cocooned inside the tiny room, with only a bench press between them. The low beat of rap music matched the pulse drumming in his wrists, his neck. "Thank you."

"Welcome." For the first time since arriving, her gaze skittered down to his bare chest and Kyler watched closely, noticing her fingers curled into her palms. Her lips rolled inward. One of her shoulders twitched, like she wanted to shrug off whatever she was feeling, but her body wouldn't quite allow it. Her tells all played out in a matter of two seconds and Kyler wished he could rewatch it over and over for the rest of his life. Hiding their attraction to one another had always been impossible. "I see you've made yourself comfortable," she said finally, her voice throatier than before.

Suspicion had Kyler narrowing his eyes. "If you came down here for a workout, you're sure as hell not dressed for it."

"I work out in leggings all the time."

"You're wearing your doctor coat."

"I..." She cleared her throat. "Have a tank top underneath."

Kyler crossed his arms and waited, laughing under his breath as vexation flashed in her eyes. Bree's hesitation was brief, before she unbuttoned the white coat and shrugged it off her shoulders. What she revealed had Kyler's cock waking up with a vengeance, straining against the front of his shorts. "That's not a tank top."

"Sports bra, tank top. Same difference." Her hands fluttered in front of the expanse of bare stomach between the white bra and the waistband of her leggings, as if wanting to cover herself. "I was running late this morning."

Drawn to his counterpart by a force stronger than himself, Kyler skirted past the bench press and stopped in front of Bree. Taking a long inhale of her crisp morning dew scent and inwardly groaning at the effect it had, he slipped a finger beneath the strap of her bra, dragging the digit over the curve of her shoulder and down the slope of Bree's back. And he circled her, watching the rise of goosebumps appear on her neck. Her back and arms. When she shivered, her head dropping forward, there was nothing Kyler could do to resist the temptation of her nape. His mouth hovered over it, breathing, but she turned and evaded before he could taste her.

Foggy brown eyes raked him. "Kyler—"

"What really brought you down here?" His tone was so low, the music nearly swallowed up his question. "I know when you're telling lies, Bree Caroline."

Her chin firmed but her eyes danced away. *Goddamn.* He *loved* her like this. Guilty and indignant. It signaled that he'd won a battle, she wasn't happy about it and would compete twice as hard next time. That fire in her stoked his own like nothing else could. Not even football.

"Karen Hawthorne was out fixing her mascara in the rearview." Bree crossed her arms and lifted her chin. "Aren't you the one who said we should be friends? Yes, yes, you did. And I was just looking out for my friend." She sniffed. "She's a viper, that one. Tried to steal Heidi's man right out from under her nose."

Kyler had nineteen female cousins and they'd haunted his house while growing up, so he considered himself pretty adept at deciphering girl code. Clearly he'd overestimated himself. "What does mascara have to do with anything?"

She shook her head at Kyler like he was a simpleton. "It means she was fixing to ask you out."

"And you didn't like that idea." Satisfaction simmered in his gut. "Gotta say, I'm beginning to warm to this conversation."

"Well, cool off. I was just being friendly."

"I could eat you up in one bite in that outfit, supergirl."

Kyler dropped his gaze just in time to watch her stomach hollow, leaving a tiny gap between her smooth belly and the waistband of her leggings. His attention dragged higher and was rewarded with the hardening of her nipples, the anxious wetting of her lips. The girl needed a good, hard ride as bad as he did. Unfortunately, she would die before admitting it, which meant a lot of finesse was required.

"Y'all, I'm going to—" Heidi popped her head around the corner, turning into the cat who caught the canary when she glimpsed Bree's attire. "I'm going to run out for an iced coffee, so I should be gone about twenty minutes. I'll be locking the door behind me, should that information be of any interest to you."

"It's not," Bree called.

"Thank you, Heidi," Kyler said at the same time.

Neither one of them moved as the lock clicked in the distance.

Chapter Seven

Shit. Almighty.

In high school, Kyler had been in great shape. Six pack, big shoulders, biceps for days, ample height without the awkwardness. The whole nine.

College had turned him from a prince into a god.

Bree went to church on Sundays, so she knew the comparison was blasphemous, but she'd ask for forgiveness later. Like when her brain cells were finished playing ping pong with her common sense. Which would not be happening with six foot four inches of brawn staring her in the face. Kyler had so many ledges, cuts, and bulges of muscle, Bree had the urge to strap on a harness and scale him like a rock climbing wall.

Too close. He was standing *way* too close. The smell of sweat and Nautica Blue climbed on board and got cozy. Lord, his calf muscles were the size of grapefruits. Those mesh shorts, riding so breathtakingly low on his pronounced hip bones, were doing exactly zero good at hiding just how *effective* her unplanned striptease had been. It hadn't been her aim to turn him on, but she definitely had. And now her own screams and moans from all those years ago were echoing in her ears like a taunt.

Kyler knew exactly how to use what lived inside his shorts. The memories of just how well were creating a weight in her tummy, pressing down, down, until wetness formed between her thighs. His parted lips and quick breaths said he knew it, too. "Don't let me keep you from your workout, Bree."

"Right," she rasped. Brushing past him, her arm grazed his ridged chest, making him groan. Bree barely resisted doing the same.

He followed her through the maze of equipment, slowly, close enough that she could hear his breaths. Her inner walls clenched tight when he made a rough sound and without turning around, she knew he was admiring her backside. *God.* God, this was a very bad situation. Closed in the tiny gym with Kyler, no one there to interrupt or distract them, if he made a move, Bree wasn't sure she had the strength to decline. It wasn't merely the fact that she'd gone four years without sex. No. It was her chemistry with Kyler, specifically. They'd gone from daily wild, desperate encounters at the creek, in his truck, behind the school…to nothing. No contact.

Her hormones were demanding she fix the way she'd slighted them. And since they hadn't been this vocal since prom night, she couldn't deny that the yearning was all for Kyler. Dammit. This was very bad. She'd made so much progress moving on.

Hadn't she?

Bree stopped at the vertical knee raise, a machine designed to work the abdomen, turned, and climbed on. Right away, she realized she'd chosen the wrong machine. It was a well-known fact that lifting your knees up to your chest while suspended sparked a down low tickle, which only increased with repetition. Throw in the scenery—her bare-chested, sexy as a motherfucker, fresh from pumping iron, aroused ex-boyfriend—and the down low tickle threatened to become a riot of lust.

"I don't need an audience," Bree managed, executing her first lift.

Kyler fastened his gaze on her stomach, where she hoped a decent flex of muscle was taking place. "Maybe not, supergirl, but you demand one." His tone was deep, sending the pulse in her neck into a flutter. A fast one. "Where were you when Heidi called?"

"I don't know what you're talking—" Bree huffed a sigh. "You knew she was going to call me, didn't you?"

He appeared to be fighting a grin. "Didn't answer my question."

"A coyote got hold of a golden retriever named Bowser." That low thrum began between her legs, intense and weighted, but she kept raising her knees, because Kyler was watching, waiting for her to say uncle and quit early. "He's going to be fine after some rest and healing."

"I've never had a chance to see you work." He didn't look happy about it, but the brooding set of his brow only made him sexier. Lift. Lift. The dull throb between her legs turned sharp, urgent. "Let me. While I'm here."

While he's here. He's leaving. "If the chance arises."

"Fine enough. For now." His tongue slid from one corner of his lips to the other. "How are these leg raises treating you? Feeling a pull anywhere?"

"Uh-uh," she said too quickly. "Nope."

"Oh no?" The next time she raised her legs, Kyler caught her beneath both knees, his movement so lightning quick she sucked in a breath, her heart flying into a chaotic hammering pace. A wicked glint flashed in Kyler's eyes. Bree didn't have a chance to decipher it before he pushed her knees higher, all the way to her shoulders, squeezing all those sensitive, aroused muscles and starting a ringing in her ears. "How about now?"

"Uh…" She gave up pretending to breathe normally, her neck ceasing to support her head. "Ky, please…"

And then she felt it. Tiny bites along the insides of her thighs, branding her through the cotton leggings. Slow, precise, *just* enough pressure. Commanding her neck to play ball, Bree looked down to find Kyler's eyelids at half mast, his white teeth sinking in every couple inches, his own chest and stomach shuddering in and out, his nipples in tight points. At the sight, the walls of Bree's core constricted and released with enough force to send a rattling gasp flying from her mouth.

"*Kyler.*"

"Bree?"

"Just…"

"Yeah." His double grip beneath her knees vanished, but before her legs could fall, Kyler was inserting his hips to catch them. One arm snaked around the base of her spine, sliding her forward and out of the machine…and then there she was. Legs wrapped around her ex-boyfriend's waist, heart pounding, moisture pooled between her thighs, their mouths separated only by a matter of an inch.

"You wore that cologne on purpose," she breathed. "Admit it."

His grin flashed. "Guilty as charged and unrepentant as a sinner."

Her gasp only widened his smile. "Bragging about sinning now, are you, Kyler?"

"You say my name all shaken up and sexy like that when you want me to kiss your pretty mouth." Hunger made his tone sound like two knives sharpening each other. "I reckon nothing has changed."

With those vivid green eyes penetrating her defenses, Bree couldn't have lied to save her life. "Yes," she whispered, her voice catching at the feel of his erection full and proud against the seam of her leggings, the warm press of his abdomen muscles at her belly. "I-in the name of being friendly and all."

Kyler rolled his hips and Bree saw stars. "It's just good manners making your pussy wet, is that right?"

"Yes?"

"Hush up, Bree."

His mouth claimed Bree's at the same time one big hand found her bottom, pulling her close, grinding their lower bodies together. And so their first kiss after four years started with an identical groan born of frustration, before it spiraled straight into madness.

Kyler wasted no time taking on the role of aggressor, his tongue sliding in to mark its territory, licking over hers once, twice, three times, before twining around it, sucking with a desperate sound, licking more.

Sensation exploded in Bree's body...but also her mind. It was like turning on a Jumbotron in a dark stadium, waking up an entire sleeping crowd and having them erupt with a foot-stomping standing ovation. Heat pulsed between her thighs, in her nipples, the sensitive areas of her neck. As if she were being touched everywhere at once, her skin kneaded by fire.

Kyler's strong hand moved in punishing efficiency on her backside, gripping her flesh tight, hefting her up when she started to slip, growling every time she re-settled on his hardness. Teasing her with low-key upthrusts designed to drive her insane. Craving a loss of control from him, ready to sell her soul for friction, Bree's legs began to move involuntarily, up and down his hips, trying to get closer, climb higher, rubbing herself on Kyler's thick flesh in the process.

"*Jesus, Bree.*" His lips slanted open over hers, released a shuddering breath right against her mouth before diving back in with barely leashed intensity. "This is how it always used to start. 'Hug me, Kyler. Keep me warm.' Soon enough, you'd have a leg around me. Didn't take long before the other one followed, did it?" They both shook their heads no, causing their lips to graze together. "No, it didn't. Now open your eyes and keep them on me while you remind me of the rest."

Bree didn't realize her eyes were closed until Kyler's words shot them open. "We'd be at the creek, most times." A lusty haze wrapped around them. "And y-you'd wait for my say-so—"

"Soon as you flashed me those eyes—you know, you *know* the hot little teasing way you did it—then I'd get on top of you, wouldn't I? Pin you down like I couldn't help it." His groan made her nipples tighten painfully. "Shit, Bree. I could barely unzip my pants and shove up your skirt, you'd have me shaking so hard."

"I'd be shaking, too," she admitted huskily, wondering if it was possible to have an orgasm just from knowing how well Kyler remembered those nights at the creek. When they were so high on each other, nothing and no one else in the world existed. Kind of like right now?

The thought might have thrown off Bree, but Kyler's tongue danced back into her mouth with enough skill to muffle it. Her fingers tingled with the need to plow through his hair and Bree obliged them, savoring the hitch in his breath. She felt the shift of control, Kyler allowing her to play. He rocked back on his heels, hips angling out to give her a sexy perch while she charted the kiss, desire detonating along her spine as his hands rode up, up and around to her breasts.

"Tell me the rest of the story," Kyler rasped at her lips. "What would happen after I'd get your skirt shoved up to your belly button? After I got a good look at your tight pussy in the moonlight?"

Bree opened her mouth to answer or moan—she had no idea which—but the response stuck in her throat when Kyler lifted her sports bra, exposing her breasts. "*Kyler.*"

With a croaked curse, he sucked one bud into his mouth, his hands sliding down to span her waist, squeezing. And he didn't let up, mouthing the tip of her breast between his lips, flickering his tongue against it. Bree could do nothing but hold on to the strands of his hair and offer herself up.

She was so lost in the oncoming rumble of a climax, she sucked in a breath at the ragged sound of his voice. "Waiting on that story, Bree. My cock is aching like a son of a bitch from having your legs around me. You've given me the look. Now you're pinned underneath me with your panties off on the creek bed." His tongue curled around her left nipple before giving it a light bite. "What happens next?"

"You'd..." The words she was about to say made her tremble, right down to her throbbing center. "You'd push yourself inside of me."

As if he thought she wouldn't have the nerve to say it out loud, his body dipped and staggered forward a step. "Had to find a different spot every week because we'd wear the grass down to nothing. From fucking on top of it. Wouldn't we, Bree?"

Oh my God. She could feel the grass beneath her now, tearing away at the roots, Kyler's hips pumping, his voice straining near her ear. "Yes."

Kyler wound a fist in her hair and tugged, his face looming above hers. "You want me to push myself up inside you right now?"

Yes, yes, yes. So close. She was *so close.* There was a good reason she should say no, but her body was in the throes of arousal so painful, tears were prickling behind her eyelids. "I-I—"

With a massive sigh, Kyler stopped rolling his body, dropping his forehead down onto hers. "That's not a yes."

She searched his heated expression up close. "I just can't...shake the feeling you want more than this from me."

Until that moment, Bree hadn't acknowledged the little voice in the back of her head telling her Kyler wasn't operating like his usual self. That his behavior was suspicious. And at her words, his green gaze sharpened. "Dinner," he said after a long hesitation. "I want dinner." His right eyebrow lifted. "Unless you're scared."

Bree dropped her legs and shoved away from Kyler, not too proud to admit she was still *dangerously* turned on. So was he. Every single inch of him. But until she figured out his angle, no way was she taking any chances letting her guard down. "All right, Ky. I'll have dinner with you."

"Yeah?"

"Yeah. Tomorrow night at my house." She fluttered her eyelashes. "My daddy will be so thrilled to see you."

Kyler narrowed his eyes, but not before she saw grudging approval drift across his face. It was a well-known fact that Bree's father was the one person in town Kyler had never won over. Probably because he'd been sneaking her out to the creek after dark since junior year and returning her home with grass stains. The fact that Bree was an active and eager participant wouldn't have mattered to Samuel Justice, though. No one was good enough for his girls and that, as they say, was that.

"I'll be there," Kyler said. "Your father still a Scotch drinker?"

"Now and again." She found her coat on the floor and put it on, determined to ignore the observance of Kyler's hungry eyes. "Bring whatever you like; it won't make a difference."

"Sounds like this calls for a bet."

Despite her better judgment, Bree's interest was piqued. "What did you have in mind?"

Kyler ambled toward her, looking like a big, sexy beast who'd had his meat dragged away before he could devour it. "If I win your daddy over this time around, you come down to the creek with me afterward."

Yearning and excitement braided together in her middle. "So your plan is to win him over, then lose favor just as fast?"

He smirked and held out his hand. "Do we have a bet?"

Again, the intuition that she was missing a piece of the bigger picture simmered in the back of her mind. But she'd never turned down a challenge from this man and wouldn't start now. She reached out and shook with Kyler, but before she could retrieve her hand, he snared her wrist. Dragged her right up against him.

"I would trade anything that happened on the field over the last four years..." He spoke in a rough whisper against her ear. "...to keep that kiss we just had from fading away. You hear me, Bree Caroline?"

Her heart rolled over and purred inside her chest. "Still a charmer, I see," Bree managed, easing past Kyler toward the exit just as Heidi returned. She muttered a hello and good-bye to her friend, prepared to leave. Before opening the door, she turned and glanced over her shoulder, finding Kyler staring after her in a way she recognized. Like she was a football about to be snapped. But his smile restored itself when he caught her looking.

Moments later, when Bree reached the sidewalk, a thought stopped her in her tracks. She'd called Kyler a charmer. As if sweet words were something that just rolled off his tongue in every direction. That wasn't true, though. It never had been.

He'd *only* ever been a charmer...for her.

Bree shook herself and kept walking. Time had changed

everything and she needed to remember that. His charm wasn't reserved just for her anymore.

But a hazy intuition continued to gnaw at her.

Along with an army of angry, thwarted hormones.

Chapter Eight

Kyler leaned against the porch rail of his family home, staring out at the surrounding cornfields and really *seeing* them for the first time in his life. When he was a child, the Tate farm was a given. The immortal place he'd been born that would never change or be taken away. Last December, however, they'd had the notion of immortality torn away when the bank attempted to repossess the land on account of late mortgage payments.

Now the cornfields looked completely different. They were more elusive. Looking at them called to mind the passage of time, the people that came before him and would come after. As he'd gotten older, a tug of war had begun inside Kyler, the farm right at the center of the rope. Football could support the people and place he loved...but pursuing the sport professionally required his absence. Required him to grow and change in a place far away from Bloomfield. Maybe even meant he would return a different man some day.

The ink was finished drying on his contract with the Rage. He'd stood on the Draft Day stage and pledged loyalty to a team. A lot like the cornfields, continuing on in the sport seemed like a given.

But not so long ago, him and Bree being together forever had seemed like a given, too. Having the rug ripped out from beneath a man brought into perspective what was important. Was it coming too late to make a difference?

Kyler's mother pulled up in her station wagon, kicking up dust on the dirt driveway. When he caught her hooded glance through the windshield, common sense told him he was in for a lecture about something. In no rush to find out what it concerned, he jogged down the steps to help with the groceries, slinging all five tote bags onto one arm. "Who's all this food for?"

"It's for *you*, Kyler. You bottomless pit son of mine," his mother huffed. "You've been eating five full meals a day since you got here, or didn't you notice?"

He thought back over the last few days and admitted silently that most of his time had been spent at the refrigerator or stove. "It's all the working out making me hungry. Sorry about that." Holding the door open for his mother, he planted a kiss on her cheek as she passed, pleased when she flushed. "You don't have to worry about me tonight. I'm having dinner with the Justices."

"Don't I know it. The news is all over town."

There it is. Kyler dropped the tote bags onto the counter, feeling his optimism sink down to the pit of his stomach. Bree would hate being the subject of gossip. As if he needed his odds of winning her back to be any lower. "Shit. Don't tell me that."

"Watch your language. And when you go closing yourself into the gym and sharing dances with a woman, you can't expect anything less. Not in Bloomfield." She busied herself emptying her supermarket haul into various refrigerator compartments. "Sandy down at Kroger—you remember her, don't you?—she's taking wagers on whether or not Samuel Justice is going to poison your dinner."

Kyler paled. "Shit. Really?"

"*Language.* And no, I'm just softening the blow." She propped an elbow on the counter, looking downright gleeful. "The wager is whether or not the town football hero will take back up with its star animal doctor."

Oh, even *better*. He could only pray Bree hadn't been in town much since he'd seen her yesterday and she'd avoided the gossip. If she started to put together why he was in Bloomfield too soon, it could blow the whole plan to hell. "Did you take any action?"

"Of course not. That would be *dis*loyal."

"You bet against me, didn't you?"

His mother didn't even have the grace to look guilty. "Only because I'm bitter." A hand went to her hip. "Honestly, Kyler. Letting me think you're home for some TLC, when all the while you're trying to sweep a girl off her feet. And didn't even let me help you." She sniffed. "Not to mention, I could have lorded this information over everyone. Now *that* is unforgiveable."

Kyler laid his cheek on top of his mother's head. "Sorry, Mom. Didn't want to jinx myself."

Another longer sniff. "I'll forgive you if I get some details."

"There's not much to say." He blew out a laugh at his understatement of the century and slumped sideways against the kitchen counter. "I need her. I love her. She's mine and I'm hers. Her stubbornness is why I love her most of all, so I'm going about this in a language only she and I know."

His mother burst into tears.

"Dad," Kyler called.

They both laughed and Kyler handed her a napkin, tugging her into the crook of his arm.

"I knew she broke your heart," his mother sobbed. "I knew you weren't over her and I don't mind saying, I didn't want you to be. That girl is special."

Hearing its name called alongside Bree's, the organ in his chest gave a hard tug. "I bet you feel pretty terrible about betting against me now."

"Almost." Her laugh was watery. "What are you bringing to dinner tonight?"

"Scotch."

Her horrified gasp could be heard three counties away. "No son of mine is showing up to dinner with liquor like some kind of social deviant." She did a quick scan of the groceries. "Give me twenty minutes and I'll have you a pie."

"I'll try not to eat more than one or two slices on the way." He winked at her warning look. "Any more suggestions?"

"Plenty." She unearthed a rolling pin from the closest drawer. "But if you only listen to one bit of advice, make it this one."

Kyler lifted his eyebrows and waited.

"I didn't raise a punk. So stop holding back and tell that girl how you feel."

Forty-five minutes later, Kyler—feeling properly chastised—drove to the Justice house in his truck, an apple pie cooling on the passenger seat. Back in Cincinnati, his teammates had always found it odd that he never got nervous before a game. Chilled as ice, he would lean against his locker and wait for Coach Brooks to deliver his speech, not a single butterfly in his stomach.

Tonight? Different story.

Not only was Kyler determined to get Bree alone tonight, but hell, he just wanted Samuel Justice to trust him. Bree loved her father and respected his opinion, so Kyler wouldn't win Bree over without his approval. Not completely. Maybe if he'd worked harder all those years ago at gaining her father's respect, she wouldn't have cut him off at the knees on prom night, revealing she wouldn't be following him to college.

With the painful memory clogging his throat, Kyler pulled up in front of the Justice house and cut the engine on his truck. Balancing the pie in one hand, Kyler climbed out. But he stopped short when Samuel Justice straightened from behind the trunk of his old silver Buick, leather briefcase in hand, and leveled Kyler with a bored look.

"Explain yourself, son."

Kyler laughed. "So much for small talk." His mother's advice from earlier came back in a tinny rush. *Stop holding back.*

Kyler thought of the cornfields. The gentle sway of the green spread out before him. All the people who'd tended to them in years past, how much purpose and routine it would take to keep them growing for eternity. Purpose swelled inside him at having been given this moment to make something lasting, like those fields. If he did it right. If he stayed true to himself and didn't allow his stride to be broken. Just like they'd fought to keep the farm, he would fight to keep Bree.

Setting down the apple pie on the hood of his truck, Kyler straightened the collar of his good shirt. "What is it you'd like to know, Mr. Justice?"

"How it's possible you're eating dinner at my table when I thought myself well rid of you four years ago?"

"Mainly because I tricked Bree into issuing the invitation. But that's not what you're asking. You want to know why I'm back in Bloomfield, haunting your dining room." Kyler glanced toward the house and caught sight of Bree moving in the indoor glow, carrying a stack of plates. "I wanted to take her out somewhere nice, but I know now that would have been a mistake. This—you and me—is a road that needs crossing."

The older man folded his arms, the briefcase still dangling in his right hand. "Why is that?"

"Because four years gave me enough perspective to know I'm nothing without her." He didn't stop to acknowledge the other man's clear surprise. "I'm back in town to make your daughter my wife. My life won't ever be complete without her. I have to believe hers won't be complete without me, either. Just for my sanity." Inside, Bree turned to look at him through the window and his pulse started knocking around. "She's not going to make this easy. Neither are you. But all due respect, sir, this time around, I'm looking forward to the test."

* * * *

Lord have mercy.

Kyler walked into her house with a face full of determination. Soon as he crossed the threshold behind her father, he sent that fortitude flying in Bree's direction and she almost had to sit down.

They hadn't been in one another's company since yesterday at the gym and she'd been plagued by hot needles of lust stabbing her at the most inopportune moments. Especially right now with those green eyes riding over her like a roller coaster car, lighting her erogenous zones up with bolts of thunder.

She'd worn *two* bras to dinner. That's how responsive her body— most noticeably, her nipples—were in Kyler's presence. Well, sitting across from her father with nipples hard enough to poke an eye out wouldn't be appropriate, would it? Thank God for her foresight because they were already reminiscing about his mouth and tongue's treatment yesterday, sitting up and begging for more attention.

Is that what Kyler's determination was all about? Getting her down to the creek after dinner to revisit old memories? Granted, those memories didn't feel in the least bit old. On the contrary, they were so fresh, she could remember them in vivid detail. As if they'd lain together on the grass as recently as today.

Since their interlude in the gym, Bree had tried to put herself into a more practical mindset. Maybe she was overthinking this situation with Kyler. They were two consenting adults with off-the-freaking-charts chemistry. He was in town for a matter of days, offering what sounded like no-commitment sex. They liked and respected one another. Why couldn't she indulge and stop worrying about what it would mean if they hooked up?

She was still asking herself that question when Kyler set down his apple pie offering on the table and leaned in to kiss her cheek. "Supergirl."

"Ky." Even after Kyler pulled back, her face tingled where his lips had touched. "Don't try and pass that pie off as your own creation. I know a Jess Tate original when I see it."

A dimple showed at the corner of his mouth. "Official taste tester is a very important job. It often goes underappreciated."

"Speaking of, I'm surprised you didn't eat half on the drive over." Flirting. She was *flirting*. In her own dining room, for heaven's sake. "Are you finally learning to control yourself?"

His voice dropped, along with his gaze, where it lingered on her double-lifted breasts. "Leaning to control myself?" He made a low sound. "Just barely."

Bree's face heated. "Kyler Joseph Tate."

"Stop tempting me when your daddy is nearby." His grin and wink sent her blood to rushing. "I've got a bet to win."

"Right. The bet."

Something about the way she said it made Kyler's smile flatten, his eyes growing troubled. "Bree—"

"Get comfortable. Dinner's almost ready."

She escaped into the kitchen, hoping she hadn't shown her hand. It was ridiculous to feel hurt by Kyler being interested in her physically. He didn't have it in him to be disrespectful. Heck, he'd shown up on time with a pie to have dinner with her father and sister. But the floor of her stomach had dropped out, half with lust, half with...disappointment soon as he made his intentions clear.

"Let me help you."

Kyler's voice in the kitchen made her pulse jump. "I've got it under control."

He hummed on his way to the stove, picking up a spoon to begin stirring. "Tell me about your day."

Bree tried not to examine the soothing heat that settled over her shoulders like warm wool. "It was a slow one, actually. Well, wait. There was one interesting patient." She bit her bottom lip to capture a smile. "A bunny rabbit came in complaining of the hiccups."

Pleasure rippled in her chest when Kyler let out a bark of laughter. "Hopped right in on his own, did he?"

"You know what I mean. His owner brought him in." She bumped him with her hip. He bumped her back. "Turned out he'd gotten out of his cage and found a puddle of spilled bubbles the kids had left around. I laid him on his back, pushed on his little belly, and a big old double bubble came right out of his mouth."

Narrowed green eyes turned in her direction. "You're making this up."

"Figured it would be more interesting than my back-to-back neutering appointments." She laughed when Kyler winced and bent forward slightly at the waist. "Men. It gets you every time."

Kyler grumbled for a few seconds until something seemed to occur to him. "So you, uh…haven't been out and about in town much since yesterday?"

"Why?"

"Just making conversation."

"Uh-huh." Bree moved closer to him, going up on her tiptoes to examine his too-casual expression. "There something I should know about?"

Kyler seemed momentarily distracted by her proximity, his Adam's apple bobbing. "Sure is." With a flick of his wrist, he turned off the burner beneath the gravy. "There's a two-for-one sale on pickles at Kroger."

"Very funny."

"One tall tale deserves another, Bree Caroline." Suddenly serious, he turned toward her and propped a hip on the stove. "Now *really* tell me about your day. I want to hear about the steps you took. If something made you laugh. Whether or not you were happy or tired or sad during any of it."

The bottom that had dropped out of her stomach back in the dining room restored itself, lifting, lifting. Pressing against her heart. When she spoke, her voice was in a whisper, like they were sharing a big secret. "I snuck out of work at lunchtime and got a pedicure while I ate a giant chocolate chip cookie." Their smiles built at the very same rate, degree by degree. "But I didn't let my polish dry enough. I never do. So my big toes have smears."

"There you go bringing up those cute toes again," he murmured back. "Let me see it."

Before she could question herself, Bree toed off her ballet flat, presenting her right foot for Kyler's inspection. "Now you know my great shame."

"Tell me I'm the only one who knows it."

His request was packed with so much gravity, Bree grew short of breath. "You are."

Kyler nodded, then reached out to slip a stray curl behind her ear. "They're taking bets in town on whether or not your daddy is planning to poison me."

"I haven't decided yet," Samuel said behind them, letting the kitchen door slam.

Bree hopped backward, ramming her hip into an open cabinet. Kyler didn't even bother taking his attention off her. In front of her father, the level of intense focus in those green eyes felt downright inappropriate, but Bree couldn't deny the pleasure spreading in her middle.

"How do I sway the odds in my favor, sir?" He paused. "Of not being poisoned, that is."

Her father hesitated a moment, which was rare for a man who so often got straight to the point, his purpose clear. "Bree, I think Kira is calling for you upstairs."

"I don't hear—" She stopped mid-sentence, realizing her father wanted to be alone with Kyler. Why? It killed her not knowing, but her father was the one human being on this planet she didn't question. "I'll go see what she needs."

At the kitchen door she looked back at Kyler, a quick rhythm starting in the center of her chest when he nodded at her. As if to say, *consider the bet won.*

Chapter Nine

Kyler knew every bump of the road leading to the creek. He steered left and right to avoid them now, but didn't quite succeed in missing them completely. His mind was in two places at once. On the girl who sat in the passenger seat looking like a lamb on the way to slaughter. And on the conversation he'd had with Samuel before dinner started.

A beat passed as the kitchen door snapped shut behind Bree.

"You want to know how to swing the odds in your favor, Mr. Tate?"

They both knew the topic of discussion had nothing to do with poison and everything to do with Bree. "Yes, sir. More than anything."

Brown eyes, a masculine version of Bree's, scrutinized Kyler. "Tell me, when did Bree decide she wanted to be a veterinarian?"

The question threw him. Hard. He'd expected the man to inquire about his cumulative GPA, medical history, or political affiliation. Panic set in upon realizing he didn't have the answer. He was not going down easy now, though, so Kyler thought hard, remembering every peak and valley he'd traveled with Bree. The occasions she'd needed time to herself. Times she'd needed extra attention from him and he'd been desperate to give it. "When her mother left."

Grief shone briefly in the older man's eyes, followed by grudging approval. "Yes. And I advise you to consider why." He tapped a fist against his thigh. "I don't make decisions for my daughter. I raised her to do that herself." Samuel started toward the door and stopped. "She puts on a good show, but she hasn't been the same since you went away. Not even close." He sighed. "In regards to what you told me outside, I won't stand in your way of trying. But I have one more condition."

It took all his willpower not to deflate into a heap of relief. "Yes, sir?"

"Get a new tie. The one you wore on Draft Day was ugly as shit."

The laughter boomed out of Kyler. "Yes, sir." He pushed himself off the counter, joining Samuel at the door and pushing it open so he could pass through. "Maybe you can take me shopping. Sounds like you have an eye for fashion."

"Don't push it."

Kyler sat down at the table, shooting an open-mouthed Bree a wink.

So Kyler should consider the night a victory, shouldn't he? Over a decade after he'd begun dating Bree, he'd finally gained Mr. Justice's favor. Or at least his assurance he wouldn't prevent Kyler from *trying* to make Bree his wife. Real reassuring. But Kyler found himself focused instead on Samuel's advice to consider the timing of Bree's decision to become a veterinarian.

Following in her father's footsteps hadn't been her passion until Mrs. Justice walked out on them. Almost immediately, she'd started accompanying her father on house calls, spending more time at the local shelter, caring for animals. Only Kyler had never considered *why*. Why was her mother leaving the catalyst?

When she'd broken up with him at the very creek to which they were driving, he'd been too devastated to look for a deeper meaning. His sole focus had been escaping the hurt and learning to live with the huge chunk losing Bree had taken out of him. A chunk that would never be filled back in, no matter how hard he tried.

But with Bree's happiness at stake, Kyler needed to examine what really held her back from coming to Cincinnati with him. And he needed to do it fast.

His flight to Los Angeles left in three days.

With that chilling fact on a repetitive loop in his head, Kyler pulled the truck to a stop at the forest's edge, rolling down the window so they could hear the gentle babble of the creek. "Here's the thing, Bree. I want you. So bad that I've been crying a little every time I zip my jeans since coming home." He turned to find a bemused expression on her gorgeous face. "But I'll be damned before I hold you to a bet where sex is my prize. I was an asshole for letting you think I'd do that." He gripped the steering wheel tight, out of annoyance at himself. "We haven't spent any real time together in a while. I shouldn't have assumed you would give me the benefit of the doubt. So what we're going to do is sit here a spell and talk.

Tomorrow, if you decide to mess up the grass with me, I'll break the speed limit coming to pick you up. But I'm happier than I've been in goddamn years just looking at you, Bree. Just to ask you things and hear your answers."

Kyler forced himself to maintain eye contact. And not to look down at the *quick quick quick* way her tits were rising and falling.

"Why'd you have to go and say all that?" she finally whispered after what seemed like an hour. "I was prepared to lay on a guilt trip."

"Sorry, supergirl." He chuckled into the near-darkness. "Go on ahead. I want whatever you've got to lay on me."

"Kyler."

"What?"

"I want to mess up the grass with you."

Talk about crying. His dick stretched up and out from the root so fast, Kyler gritted his teeth with a curse. "Tomorrow, Bree," he managed, stars shooting in front of his eyes. "When it's clear you're not fulfilling your end of some stupid challenge."

Bree shook her head. "Our challenges aren't stupid; they're exactly what we both need." She blinked, as if the admission had surprised her, too. "Maybe we should have another one right now."

Hope waved its flag on the horizon, but he staunchly ignored it. "I'm listening, but I'm not making any promises."

"Let's start with a clean slate."

She turned her body, sliding her bent left knee up onto the seat. *Don't look for that sweet flash of panties. Don't do it.* "A clean slate," he rasped. "I'm with you so far."

"There was never a bet to win my father over." Bree scooted closer and Kyler held his breath. "How you accomplished that is still a mystery, but that explanation is for another time. Right now, we're getting a do-over." She unhooked his seatbelt, the zip-reel sound going straight through him. "Dare me to turn you down."

He caught her hand before it could settle on his chest. "You're not hearing me. I'm turning myself down on your behalf."

"Come on, Kyler. If you dare me to turn you down, I'll be obliged to do the opposite." She twisted her hand out of his grip, curling those long, graceful fingers of hers in his collar. "It's how we do things."

Christ, having Bree so close was mental damnation and salvation, all at once. She was crumbling his resistance little by little, but he didn't want her on a technicality. "That's not how we're doing things tonight." He brought their foreheads together, let his tongue slide out and meet with her lower lip. "No games, Bree. Say you need me."

With the ultimate challenge lying between them, brown eyes traced up to lock with his. "You're not making this easy, are you?"

"What's holding you back from saying it?"

Time slowed down, the watery bubbling of the creek fading out. "The worry that it might be true."

Kyler's heart went wild in his chest, hammering so fast his vision tripled. His hands shook. The light she'd blown out inside him flamed brighter than ever, a fireworks display inside his chest. Bree, however, looked like a frightened deer in a hunter's sights. She attempted to throw herself back toward the passenger side of the truck, but Kyler wasn't letting her go now. Oh no. She'd finally said what he'd known in his bones since day one, all the way back in middle school.

Their need went both ways. It was solid, immeasurable, and couldn't be weakened by absence or the passage of time.

"Get over here, Bree Caroline." Kyler grabbed her around the waist, hauling her back across the seat and out of the truck. She was in his arms before she could form a protest, but she certainly made a show of sputtering as he strode with her toward the creek. "Go on, then. Now that you've given me the truth, I'll let you complain a little. Right before I lick it straight out of your mouth."

"You..." she started in a shaky whisper. "Y-you're..."

"Sad. Happy. Horny. Miserable. Confident. Worried. Horny. Did I say that last one twice?" As soon as he reached the grassy bank surrounding the creek, Kyler dropped to his knees with Bree still cradled in his arms. And then she was on her back beneath him, twin reflections of the moon lighting up her eyes. "*You.* You make me everything on that fucking list."

"Oh yeah?" Baring her teeth, she took hold of either side of his shirt and ripped it straight down the middle, sending buttons flying in every direction. "If I make you so crazy, what do you want with me?"

"*Everything.*"

Chapter Ten

Shit.

Almighty.

The kiss Kyler dropped on Bree almost sent her into a blackout. A lust-driven, not-in-control-of-her-limbs, shot-into-another-dimension loss of awareness.

His teeth nipped around her lower lip, dragging it down, leaving her mouth vulnerable so he could lay claim. With his tongue. His lips. And Lord, did he ever. It was the kiss that wouldn't stop giving. Just a wet, writhing, slanting mating of mouths and at some point, Bree gave up on the act of breathing. If she died this way, she wouldn't even feel death creeping in because she was too busy being consumed by Kyler. His kiss was wild, frustrated, giving, desperate. She felt everything inside her expand in the presence of it, threatening to burst.

Bree's body must have acted out of self-preservation, pulling on the roots of Kyler's hair until he broke the kiss, allowing her to suck in deep, labored pulls of oxygen. His face was hard to see in the shadows, but worry for her made his eyes an intense green, his lips descending once more. But not for another kiss. No, he fit their mouths together and breathed. Breathed again.

"What is this?" Bree murmured, voice catching. "Some sexy version of CPR?"

His lips curved briefly against hers. "We should trademark it. I might be on to something." Once again, he gave her a slow dose of air and sensual languidness slithered through Bree's body. "Nah, I'm keeping it just for you."

Maybe it was the additional oxygen. Or maybe it was just the intimacy of the act itself. But her body stretched out and arched beneath Kyler's, her thighs opening and inviting him to drop down. To push. To pin. Her body was a begging mass of nerve endings screaming for an anchor. "*Kyler.*"

"Shh, I'm coming." Bracing one hand beside Bree's head, he gave her the full weight of his lower body, hissing when her warmth welcomed the thick flesh behind the zipper of his jeans. As if his body was operating on pure animal need, he thrust once, driving her a few inches up the creek embankment. "This what you're impatient for?"

"*Yes.* I…"

"Tell me, Bree. Tell me everything."

"Say you need me back."

Oh *God.* Where had *that* come from? Now it was a competition to see what would burst into flames first—her face or her body. It didn't help when Kyler stared down at her like she needed a straightjacket. "Bree, I'm a mess. I've been a mess since the last time we stood beside this creek. You want to know if I need you? Just look at me. All you ever have to do is look at me and you'll see it."

Bree used a mental machete to slash a pathway out of her head… And once she stood on the other side, it was like stumbling into a vivid, Technicolor dream. So much pent-up passion ran circles in Kyler's eyes, she couldn't believe she hadn't seen it before. At least not since he'd come home to visit. "Oh." She swallowed hard. "You *are* a mess."

He dropped his face into the crook of her neck and rolled those powerful hips, denim dragging over cotton, enticing the flesh beneath. "Heal me. Please."

Responsibility and a renewed wave of desire moved inside Bree. Following instinct, she urged Kyler to roll onto his back, leaving her straddling his lap. Now that she'd slipped into the land of Technicolor, her senses were so sharp, so attuned to this man, she heard his fingers digging into the earth, heard the *whap whap whap* of his heart.

Need her? This snapping connection between them went beyond need. And there was no denying it right now. Not with him in pain beneath her. Pain she was driven to relieve, the urge to do so stronger than anything she could remember. Her own desire more than matched Kyler's, swelling with every passing moment.

Bree gathered the hem of her dress and whipped off the garment, turning slippery between her thighs when Kyler groaned, his hips lifting and falling beneath her. A raring engine. Glorying in his hunger, Bree unhooked the front of her bra, removing it in a slow tease. But she stopped short when Kyler's eyebrows drew together. "How come you took off your bra, but you've still got one on?"

"Oh th-that." She got busy unhooking the second bra. "Would you believe it was an honest mistake?"

His lips jumped at one corner. "Nope."

"I didn't want my hard nipples showing at dinner. You happy?"

"Blissful." Her exposed breasts got rid of the grin on his face. "Bree Caroline, you are the most beautiful woman on the goddamn planet."

Bree's pulse thudded in her temples, the base of her neck, between her legs. If she basked too long in Kyler's devouring gaze, surely she would explode, so she slipped back on his thighs, her fingers working to unzip his pants. She couldn't stop herself from stealing glances at him, though, his huge, chiseled body lying there in the grass, waiting to give pleasure.

By the time she finally held his thick shaft in her hand, Kyler's breath had grown labored, sweat beginning to dapple his heaving chest. "You've still got those little red panties on, Bree. Come on up here so I can get them off."

Urgency pumping in her veins, she stroked Kyler, struggling to come up with a plan that didn't involve her climbing off him, because that would suck. The only plan she was interested in was seating herself on that hard part of him and riding him until they were both mindless. "I think...I think I can slide them down."

"Uh-uh. You know what I want." He crooked a finger at her. "We both know I won't go in smooth without giving you a good licking first. So come on up here and get it. Want your gorgeous thighs around my face."

Kyler didn't give her a chance to follow his instructions, grabbing her by the hips and hauling her up, up, until the material of her panties was stretched just above his mouth. Bree fell forward, planting her palms on the grass, whimpering when Kyler's warm breath heated the sensitive insides of her thighs. The sound of the creek rushed in her ears, interrupted only by the sounds of cotton ripping, a guttural groan. Lips met her damp flesh almost immediately and Kyler's hands returned to her hips only to press them down, meeting the most sensitive part of her with the flat of his tongue. Rubbing it there.

"Oh, that's *oh*..." The summer evening dew on the grass made Bree's knees slip wider. *That* and the fact that they were trembling out of control. "I'm not going to make it. I'm going to..."

Apparently Kyler wasn't listening, because he continued to mete out torture, massaging her hips and buttocks in his calloused hands, slipping his tongue up and back through her folds, teasing her nub endlessly until Bree's cheek was grinding against the soft ground, her hips rolling toward the only thing that could end the pain. Every delicate and neglected muscle south of her belly button began to converge in on itself, constricting, stealing the breath right out of her lungs. But just as she bit down on her bottom lip and readied herself to field the orgasm of the century, she heard the sound of foil ripping. Then in one hasty, hungry move, Kyler used his grip on Bree's hips to lift her up, repositioning her on his lap.

"Need you, Bree. *Need you.*"

His hand shifted between her thighs, brushing her flesh, and she let out a sob. The head of his erection met her entrance and they locked eyes, Kyler's the definition of starvation. Enough to humble Bree, start a rhythm in her chest she wasn't sure would ever stop. "Need you, Kyler."

Bracing her hands on his chest, Bree filled herself with Kyler's hard length, gasping from the pressure. The incredible, mind-blowing pressure. She let her gaze sweep over the straining cords of his neck, the shuddering lift and fall of his stomach, the desperate grip spanning her waist. *Everything is right where it's supposed to be*, said a voice in the back of her mind.

Not even the sky falling could have prevented her from moving in that moment. From twisting her hips back, lifting to the plump head of his shaft, and rolling back down. A dance that was somehow singular to them and old as time, all at once. That first downward grind had Kyler throwing his head back and releasing a satisfied shout. Which was when Bree remembered why they'd always found it necessary to drive out to the creek to make love.

"We never did this quietly, did we?"

Kyler's voice sounded just as unnatural as hers when he responded. "A man can't stay silent when he's wrapped up in something so tight." His thumb rubbed over her clitoris, side to side. "Christ, I thought my mind had exaggerated how good you feel, Bree. How good *we* feel. It's taking everything I got not to flip you over and *ram* myself—" He cut himself off with gritted teeth, eyes closing. "No, I'm going to make this last. I want this to go on forever. You sitting there, full of my inches, thighs dancing around like you can barely handle them."

"Forever might be a stretch if you keep talking like that," she managed on a shaky inhale, her hips bucking involuntarily.

"Ride it, Bree," he gritted, levering his hips up for a long, slow grind. "Been too damn long since I came with my cock inside you and not just imagining it there."

Her pulse stuttered. "Did you imagine it a lot?"

"*Every. Time.*"

Something worrisome tugged on Bree's subconscious, but she could only focus on the pressure mounting inside of her. The incessant quickening that built higher every time she snapped her hips, Kyler's thickness pumping in and out of her wet heat. The base of him grazed her clitoris every time she moved, but Kyler—who she'd often suspected knew her body better than she did—pressed down on the small of her back, creating an angle that made her climax loom like an inferno.

"Oh my God." She let out a broken sob. "*Yes.*"

"There's my girl now. Who knows what you like?" His thumb joined the base of his erection in stroking the sensitive spot, his eyes glittering up at her in the darkness. Encouraging her to come apart, to take what she needed. "Spent the best hours of my life learning your needs, making sure you'd always finish first. Got my girl's slippery-wet pussy memorized, don't I?"

When his hips started giving quick upward thrusts, his thumb moving in a blur, Bree dug her fingernails into Kyler's pectorals and screamed, the pleasure reaching into her belly pulling everything *tight, tight, tight.*

Releasing.

Kyler shoved up deep and Bree pressed down, working as a team without exchanging a single word to give her the longest peak, and it went on and on until her voice started to go hoarse from calling his name. Her legs clamped around Kyler's hips like he was the only raft in a storm. In a way he was because Bree swore she'd been struck by lightning.

"Missed you clinging to me most of all, didn't I?" Kyler said through gritted teeth. "Only time I know you won't run off is when I'm giving you a good fucking. You stay put for that, don't you?"

Without giving her a chance to recover, without giving her the sweet kisses and reassurances of their youth, Kyler turned them a final time, settling Bree on her hands and knees in the grass. Bree stared out into the moonlit trees as Kyler dragged his hot open mouth up her spine and buried his face in her neck, sounding like a man who'd just swum from the bottom of the ocean without an oxygen tank.

One of his knees slid in between her thighs, prying them wide. That hard, heavy part of him filled her in a rough shove. And, groaning into her shoulder, one hand fisted in her hair, he fucked her into next week.

"Slide your ass up my stomach. I've got a few more inches to give you." His answering curse was followed by her name, and satisfaction flowed hot in her blood, dizzying her. "Dammit, Bree, that's so fucking good. Now push, push back…*Jesus*. You have no idea what you do to me. What you've *always* done. *No idea*."

She started to slide forward in the grass, but he jerked her back with a forearm beneath her hips. "Oh God," she whimpered. "*Harder*."

"There it is." His growl sent shockwaves through her blood. "There's our magic word. My harder's a little different this time around, though. You want it?"

"*Yes*."

The impact of his lower body spurring into a ruthless pace made Bree suck in a ragged breath, her flesh quickening around him. Her vision started to glaze with another oncoming wave of pleasure, teeth beginning to chatter in her mouth. Behind her was not the boy who'd spent countless hours in that very spot learning her body, teaching her about his. No, this was Kyler Tate the *man*. A rough, demanding man that couldn't achieve release without *her* and that very thought alone, coupled with his groans, spurred her into another mind-blanking orgasm.

"Kyler. *Kyler*."

"So sweet. You're so fucking sweet and snug, Bree, shaking around me. I can't hold it back anymore. Too long. It's been too long."

His husky ramble hitched in her ear, followed by a long moan, the broken pumping of his hips. Those strong arms banded around her, supporting her, but also crushing her up into his body. One final thrust and they both went down into the grass, Kyler's arms breaking her fall as he shuddered through his peak. "Bree," he breathed finally, his body going limp, laying partially on top of her. "My girl."

It took a few minutes for the fog to part. Bree almost wished it wouldn't, wished they could go on lying there together all night, not thinking about a single thing. Except for the fact that they'd surely just raised the bar on sex between humans. Because holy damn. She was going to feel it for a week and she didn't even mind.

Her heart wouldn't let her rest, though. No, it walked right upstairs to her brain and knocked on the door, tapping its foot until it was acknowledged.

At some point during the night, she'd forgotten all about what was bothering her. Kyler was leaving in a matter of days. Which made tonight nothing more than a hookup. A pit stop on his way to Los Angeles. And while Bree wished she was the kind of woman who could appreciate sex for sex's sake... The increased discomfort in her sternum was making it painfully obvious that sex with Kyler had never, ever, just been about sex. Although, that wasn't the case for Kyler, was it?

You broke my heart. I went away and healed it up. Now we're going to be friends.

Just friends. A visit with an old flame.

For him, anyway. In the blink of an eye, Bree was right back where she'd started the day Kyler left for Cincinnati. Alone. Missing him so bad she could barely perform basic functions like walking or tying her shoes. No way to fix the ache and remain true to what she loved. Who she was. Her options were even more limited this time around because tonight was purely physical for Kyler.

"All right, supergirl. Smoke is about to come out of your ears." He dropped a kiss onto her nape, bundled her closer. "Tell me what's wrong."

"I thought, um..." Her voice was doing that super high-pitched thing that always betrayed her when she got overwrought. "I thought I would be okay with just, like, hooking up, but it turns out I'm not. Not okay with being your hookup."

Kyler tensed up behind her. *Jerk.* He was probably regretting bringing her down to the creek in the first place, thinking she'd gone all psycho ex-girlfriend on him. Wanting more when he no longer did.

That distressing thought had Bree attempting to scramble out of Kyler's arms, but he held on tight. "How dare you get weird on me, Kyler Joseph? I'm not asking you to go steady. I'm just…I'm *just*…" To Bree's horror, tears pricked the back of her eyelids, lost the battle to stay contained, and slipped down her cheeks. "Maybe I could have handled this kind of thing better with someone else—"

"What the hell are you talking about, *someone else?*"

"Maybe it wouldn't have felt this *awful* afterward," she shouted back, finally succeeding in breaking free, reaching out to snag her dress. Oh God, she had to get home. Something was wrong with her. Her foundation felt like it was cracking straight down the middle. "You were honest with me, so I-I guess I shouldn't be mad. But this doesn't feel like us. We hook up a-and then you leave? This doesn't feel like the us we used to be. I'd rather remember us like we were."

Dress pulled on, Bree finally turned toward Kyler and saw his face. He stood a few yards away, breathtaking and bare-chested in the moonlight, his boxers pulled back into place. His face was paler than the orb lighting the forest, but when he saw her tears, devastation rippled over his features.

"This is what I get for holding back," he whispered.

Chapter Eleven

At what point in his life would he realize his mother was always right? The possible repercussions of what he'd just done socked Kyler in the stomach, one after the other, as if he were standing in front of a fast pitch machine without a bat.

"Bree, please." He took a step forward and she retreated, increasing his panic. "Please don't cry."

"This is what you get for holding back. What does that mean?"

Kyler dropped his head into his hands. Where the hell did he begin? "I can't get my thoughts together when you're crying."

"Try harder."

He rasped a sound. Shit, the more he concentrated, the worse his reality became. He'd been deceptive. Maybe he'd considered playing it close to the vest necessary to his plan, but sleeping with Bree when he hadn't been honest? That behavior was inexcusable and now… Now the love of his life thought the worst. Thought he'd brought her to this place that held so many memories just to get his rocks off. Well, he could clear that nonsense right up.

Unfortunately, the truth could send Bree jumping into the creek, doing a freestyle stroke to get away from him. Too bad. He'd landed himself in that same creek with no paddle and now he owed her an explanation. God, he'd sell his soul right now to stop her tears.

Without taking his gaze off Bree longer than necessary, Kyler stooped down to retrieve his shirt, pulling it on. First off, if she ran, he didn't want to chase her naked. Second, a man ought to have his nipples covered when a woman's claws came out. "I'm asking you to take what you know about me, Bree. Take what you *know* and apply it to this situation."

Bree's swiped at her damp eyes. "I don't understand."

"Think. Think about senior year when the fall carnival came to town. You remember that?" Her nod was hesitant. "I emailed the director two months in advance asking him to let us in an hour before everyone else on opening day. I emailed him and made phone calls until he caved. All because you loved the Ferris wheel and I wanted you to be the first one to take a ride. You remember that?"

She crossed her arms. "Are you trying to buy yourself points here?"

"No, I'm trying to remind you that I'm a planner." He took another step in her direction, thankful when she stayed put. "Think, Bree. Do you really believe I would come to Bloomfield unannounced, show up at the dance, and risk being poisoned by your daddy...just to hook up with you? Not that touching you, kissing you again, wouldn't be worth all that work and a lot more, supergirl, but you know me better than that." Tension was beginning to creep into her frame, so Kyler took that final step to bring them toe to toe. "You know I want more with you, Bree Caroline. You know I want it all. And I'm not going to stop until I get it."

A little puff of air passed through her lips, thoughts zigzagging behind her eyes. "I—what?" Her swallow sounded more like a *thunk*. "You said you went away and healed."

"That was the biggest lie I told you." Of their own accord, his hands slipped around her upper arms and held fast. "You broke my heart. And it's *still broken*." Saying the truth out loud after keeping it penned up for so long started flames licking inside his blood, sending gray smoke whirling inside his head. "I've loved you as far back as my memory reaches. I will *never* fucking stop. I came to town for one damn reason, Bree. So I could leave here with my wife. You."

"Kyler," she breathed, her cheeks growing more and more damp, every tear doing its best to slay him. "That's...crazy. We haven't been together in four years."

Holding back or being delicate was out the window. Cinder and ash and truth poured out of him, scorching him on the way out. "And yet I've been faithful. My hands are meant for you alone and I haven't laid them on a single other person." He held them up, palms out, as if the proof was visible. "Tell me you haven't been faithful right back, so

I can kiss your lying mouth."

When she didn't respond, Kyler had his answer and relief melted in his gut.

"You're *my* girl. You always have been." His voice shook. "That's why you run and hide every time I come to town, because your heart wouldn't let you forget it."

He watched as she desperately searched for a defense. "You didn't exactly come find me, either."

"I wasn't ready, Bree. I was still angry. At you for cutting me off. At myself for not being good and smart enough to keep you." She made a sound and looked away. "Now I'm only angry over how much time has passed. I forgive us both. But I can't make it without you. I got called to the stage on Draft Day and all I could think about was you. How none of it meant shit unless you were standing beside me."

It made him want to tear out his hair, the disbelief she turned on him. "This is my home, Kyler. Nothing has changed. I won't leave it or my family."

"Well, *you're* my home and I won't leave you behind, either." He shook her a little, knocking tears free of their perch on her eyelashes. "There are some things I missed last time we stood in this spot. You've got reasons for not wanting to give up this life to start a new one with me, the way we planned. I'm going to learn every one of those reasons." Kyler braced himself. "But right now, I just need you to tell me you still love me. Tell me you never stopped."

The war that went on inside Bree was beautiful. She sobbed and blinked through it, words being formed and discarded on her kiss-swollen lips. "You know I hate surprises, Ky. You can't just come here and *spring* this on me. E-expect me to tell you what you want to hear. If I'd known you wanted to get back together... If you'd told me the truth—"

"We wouldn't be standing here. So I can't regret it." Forcing himself to breathe through the agony and disappointment, Kyler used the hem of his shirt to wipe her cheeks. "Only thing I regret is making you cry."

"I feel like I'm hurting you all over again." She batted his hands away, wrapping her arms around her middle. "Why are you doing this?"

"You're hurting, too." Banking the urge to hold her and refuse to let go, he pointed back to the spot where they'd made love. "That feeling you got afterward? The one that said me leaving was wrong? That's fate trying to tell you something, Bree. I'm begging you to listen."

"I won't leave," she whispered.

His heart twisted. "Look me in the eye, Bree Caroline." He stepped closer so she wouldn't have a choice, her head falling back to maintain his gaze. "I won't leave this town without you."

Knowing Bree as long as he had, Kyler knew when she'd gone her maximum number of rounds. No decisions or resolutions were going to be made tonight, or even tomorrow, because his girl was a thinker. A brooder. After the shit he'd been pulling all week, Kyler reckoned he owed her some stewing time, much as staying away from her would be pure, punishing torture.

"Come on, supergirl." He kissed her forehead. "I'll drive you home."

He'd waited four years. He'd wait a hundred more.

* * * *

Bree snapped her supply bag shut and took a deep breath.

Two days was long enough to be holed up in the house.

Who was she kidding? It hadn't been *nearly* long enough. She was still reeling from Kyler's confession and that wouldn't be changing any time soon.

He still loved her.

He'd been faithful.

He wasn't leaving Bloomfield without her.

Bree from the past was somewhere laughing like a lunatic, because Bree of the present had broken the cardinal rule when it came to Kyler Tate. She'd let her guard down. Growing comfortable in the past had led to sunrise Ferris wheel rides, gifts left inside her locker, taps on her window at night.

Growing up, a lot of people had underestimated Kyler. He looked the part of a man who was treated to surprises and pleasure from *others*. A man who had things handed to him. Not the other way around. But the gorgeous football god had never failed to amaze her. Somehow she'd forgotten—and once and for all been knocked straight back onto her ass.

Grateful for the silent house, Bree sat down on the bench in the entryway, applying pressure to the center of her chest. She felt winded. Every time she got a burst of energy, she would think of Kyler's pleading eyes, his familiar face outlined by the night sky, and she would ache. *Ache*. Almost like she'd suppressed the misery for four years and was only now allowing it to manifest.

She looked across the hall at the family portrait hanging there. Her mother sat at the forefront, Samuel's hands on her shoulders, Bree at her side, Kira on her knee. There was a distant look in the woman's eye, as if she'd been dreaming about some far-off place. Tahiti, Berlin…Los Angeles. Every time Bree passed the picture, she forced herself to look at it. Used it as a reminder to be satisfied with what she'd been given. In Bloomfield with her family, she was happy. Content.

There was nothing more to it.

When she stood up, bag in hand, the uncomfortable throbbing remained in her chest, but she ignored it, pushing out the front door.

Kyler stood on the porch, his eyes weighed down with dark circles.

"Bree," he said, his voice a husky scrape.

Her heart picked up into a gallop. "Ky."

They stood there for a full minute, listening to the rain fall softly on the eaves above. Lord, Kyler had been right about one thing. She'd avoided him every time he came to Bloomfield because the sight of him affected her like nothing else could. Her mouth dried up, her pulse creating a racket. Now that she knew he still loved her, it took all of her willpower to keep her knees from buckling. The power of his emotions was so thick, reaching out and curling around her.

But what about her own? Had she spent so long convincing herself she was getting over him that she'd succeeded?

Her heart didn't seem to think so. Not in the slightest.

Bree thought of the picture hanging in the entryway and squared her shoulders. "I'm sorry. I haven't changed my mind."

The wattage of his gaze dimmed, but he nodded. "Where are you headed?"

"House call."

"Mind if I come with?"

"I certainly do." She took the umbrella out of her bag, opening it. "It wouldn't be very professional of me to show up with an audience."

"Doubt anyone in Bloomfield would mind."

"The appointment isn't in Bloomfield."

Bree recognized her mistake when Kyler's brows slashed inward. "Where?"

Schooling her features, she breezed past him down the stairs. "Hashtown."

Kyler was hot on her heels. "This wouldn't happen to be the trainer that keeps asking you out, is it?" He slapped a hand on the driver's side door to keep her from opening it. She gasped when he aligned their bodies from behind, pressing her up against the car. His mouth found a sensitive spot on her neck and stayed there, his warm breath coasting into her hair, down the collar of her T-shirt. "You wouldn't want to drive me stark raving mad like that, would you, Bree?"

"Not on purpose," she whispered. "There's a mare about to foal. The horse trusts me and I want to be there."

"Have some *mercy* on me," he enunciated. "And let me come *with* you."

"Fine," she said, his urgency cutting through her reservations. "Yes. Okay."

When he took away the heat of his body, the weight of it, Bree no longer felt tethered to the ground. After taking a moment to compose herself, she turned to find Kyler growing increasingly soaked by the rain, droplets running down his face and bare arms, the white T-shirt he wore clinging to his muscular chest. A chest that started a rapid rise and fall when he caught her looking. "What other mercies can I earn from you today?" Kyler rasped. "If you've already forgotten how I beg for that mercy, my tongue is dying to show you."

When he came close once more and stopped a mere inch away, her nipples tingled, making her wish she'd worn a second bra again. Especially when his gaze swept down and made blatant promises to the traitors. "Kyler—"

"Shhh." He dropped his head down and grazed wet, masculine lips over hers, sending her ovaries into chaos. One hand rose to bury in the hair at her nape, tilting her head to one side. Then, slowly, he raked that hot, open mouth up the side of her neck. "Just let me soak you up."

"Soak me up," she repeated, her nerve endings going wild.

He hummed in the affirmative, letting their hips meet and press so she could feel his thick need against her belly. "Soak you up." His tongue traced a path up to her ear, creating an answering tug between her legs. "Hell, just *soak* you. In both of us. I'm full to aching. Don't tell me you aren't after that reminder of what we've been going without."

Bree almost succumbed and let Kyler have her, right there against the truck, because hell yes, she'd been replaying their night at the creek on mental repeat. Now wasn't the time, though. Not while they were smack dab inside a gray area with no resolution in sight. Furthermore, didn't she have a job to do in Hashtown? An important one? "I-if you're going to come with me, there's no touching." His jaw tightened until she thought it might shatter, but after a few seconds he stepped back, lifting his hands in surrender. Buried beneath his hunger, there was a hint of that boyish chagrin from her best memories and Bree was hit with a wave of nostalgia so strong, it made her knees tremble. She knew this man so well. Knew him right down to the very core. Always had. "I want to be your friend, Ky. Like you said outside the diner, on your first day back." She shook her head. "I'm sorry I hid from you."

Surprise flickered in his expression, but Bree could tell it was nowhere close to what he wanted to hear. "I'm sorry, too." His throat worked a moment, before he circled to the passenger side of her truck and climbed in, watching her through the rain dappled glass.

This was going to be a long afternoon.

Chapter Twelve

Being jealous was a first.

In the past, Kyler had always been possessive in the sense that he enjoyed letting people know the following: Bree belonged to him, he made her happy, and no one else need apply. But Bree never once gave him cause to be actively jealous and vice versa. A pretty rare feat among high school students. Kyler was damn grateful now that they'd been the exception to the rule because it meant Bree trusting his word without question when he said he'd been faithful.

Bree hadn't dated, either, so there was no reason to feel edgy and irritable. He didn't like the fact that she'd been asked out at all, though. Kind of felt like his tonsils were being yanked out with pliers. Not a nice sensation.

Hell, it didn't surprise him one bit that another man had taken notice of Bree. Big, beautiful bedroom eyes and a mouth that could snap out a comeback faster than lightning tended to get attention. Throw in that fluid, sexy way she walked, her grace, her intelligence? Kyler should count himself lucky someone else hadn't gotten the notion to propose to her while he was in Cincinnati.

Realizing his fingers were digging into the meat of his thighs, Kyler forced himself to rein in the green monster.

"This is a bad idea," Bree muttered, casting him a speculative look from the driver's seat. "You're an animal skin toga away from turning into a caveman."

"You want to see me in leopard print." He winked at her. "Hint taken."

Bree's laugh tinkled like jostled bells. "You're forgetting I already have."

The memory came back to him in a series of sounds and blurry pictures. "Valentine's Day. That's right." Wrapping paper tearing. Bree squealing as he tickled her ribs, the present resting on the floor beside them. "You always were creative when it came to giving gifts."

"I knew I couldn't beat you at being thoughtful, so I went for cheap laughs instead." Turning the truck off the road, she bit her lip. "You still have those leopard print boxers?"

"I have everything you've ever given me."

Her eyelids fell, silence filling the car for long moments. "I lived in fear of my father finding those boxers before I could give them to you." A small smile formed on her mouth. "Afterward, I lost sleep wondering if your mama would find them. You promised me to hand-wash them in the sink, so she wouldn't."

Kyler scratched his chin and braced for impact. "About that..."

Bree gasped, jerking the wheel of the truck. "Kyler Joseph Tate."

"I accidentally put them in the laundry basket once. Came home to find them neatly folded on my pillow." He shook his head. "My mom has a weird sense of humor."

"How am I ever going to look her in the eye again?"

An image of Bree and his mother sitting side by side at a dinner table made him yearn so hard, he had to take a few seconds to breathe. "You ever bump into my mother around town?"

"Don't think I'm letting the subject slide."

"Wouldn't dream of it, supergirl."

She sent him some hefty side-eye, but softened when Kyler pasted on his most contrite expression. "Once in a while at Nelson's. She's usually there with friends having coffee and pie." A beat passed. "She always asks me if I'm seeing anyone."

"And you always say, 'No, ma'am. Just textbooks and the backs of my eyelids.'"

Bree stretched her fingers on the steering wheel. "Should have known she was asking for you."

"Got the full report every Sunday." They traded a turbulent glance. "You want to know what really got it in my head, Bree? That I needed to come get you back?"

"I, um..." The pulse fluttered at the base of her neck, her body shifting in the driver's seat. "I don't know, I—"

"While you decide, I'll get started. How about that?" Kyler looked straight out the windshield toward the approaching farm, but in his mind's eye, he saw a man standing on his family's porch, cornfields spread out behind him. "You remember back in December when we almost lost the farm?"

She took one hand off the steering wheel and placed it over her heart. "Thank God you didn't."

"Yeah." Kyler swallowed the tightness in his throat. "Coach Brooks's girlfriend, Peggy—she's his wife now—came up with the fundraiser to satisfy the debt we owed to the bank. Well, it turned out Peggy and Brooks dated on the sly once upon a time. And while they were in Bloomfield, he was working on getting Peggy back. Failing pretty hard at it, best I could tell."

He laughed under his breath at the memory of his coach, living legend Elliott "Kingmaker" Brooks asking for dating advice on his porch.

"So I told him to take her to Marengo Cave." Kyler couldn't stop himself from grinning. "You remember when we went there?"

"I remember the bats."

"That can't be the *only* thing you remember." Taking a chance, Kyler reached across the console and laid a hand on Bree's thigh, groaning inwardly when the muscles twitched beneath his palm. "If I recall correctly, that was one of those times you couldn't keep these babies from cinching up around my waist."

With trembling fingers, Bree cranked the air conditioner, giving him an evil look when he chuckled. "I was scared of having my blood sucked out."

"All part of my diabolical plan." Giving her thigh one final squeeze, Kyler took his hand back. "I told my coach about you and he said something that stuck. Stuck harder than I realized at the time. 'Imagine you have one more day to fix everything…before she never thinks about you again.'" A chill moved through him and it had nothing to do with the air conditioner. "Scared the shit out of me, Bree. Still does. I didn't know how much until I was drafted."

She pulled the truck to a stop outside a freshly painted barn, her hand falling limp after turning off the ignition. "There's nothing that could stop me thinking about you. Our pasts are twined too closely together for that."

"You could say the same about our futures."

Her breath caught and the moment slowed down, Bree turning soft eyes on him, rain pattering on the truck's roof. In that space of time, he saw past her defenses. Saw they were weakening. And for the first time since coming back to Bloomfield, he reckoned he might have a chance.

"Kyler."

"I know I'm pushing, but I'm running short on time, Bree." Instinct screamed at him to drag her into his lap, to kiss the reservations and doubts out of her mind, but now wasn't the time. If he moved forward before she caught up, he'd ultimately lose ground, and that was out of the question.

His flight was scheduled for tomorrow afternoon.

The sound of the barn door sliding open had both of them looking out the windshield. A man who looked to be in his mid-twenties strode out through the opening, a cowboy hat shielding his head against the rain. His smile was wide when it searched out Bree in the truck, but it dimmed when he saw Kyler. *Good.*

"Behave yourself, Kyler Joseph, or I'll take a bite out of you."

"Promise?"

Color deepening on her cheeks, Bree collected her bag and climbed out of the truck, waving at the approaching fuck-face. "Hey, Mitch. How's the patient?"

"Mitch," Kyler snorted, then went to join them outside.

Kyler's competitive side could be fierce when the situation called for it. During his final year at Cincinnati, he'd been one of the three team captains, putting him at centerfield for the coin toss. No matter how often football purists waxed poetic about sportsmanship, that strut down the fifty-yard line to size up the opposing team's captains called for intimidation. Always had. While some of his teammates liked to crack their necks or bash their shoulder pads, Kyler chose to stand real still and make eye contact with each opposing player, looking for chinks in their armor. If he were the bragging sort, he'd call it damned effective.

This situation with Mitch wasn't a competition, though. He wasn't trying to be the bigger, more intimidating man. If he handled his jealousy by acting like a territorial dick, Bree would shut down on him faster than he could spit. So while the green monster hummed and shook inside him, begging to be appeased, Kyler forced himself to ignore it and remember one thing.

A life with him in Los Angeles was Bree's choice. Not his. He'd laid his cards on the table, bared his feelings, and the next move belonged to her. All he could do at this point was surprise her. And God knew, he loved doing that.

"Good to meet you, Mitch. Kyler Tate." He put his hand out. "Hope you don't mind me tagging along to watch Bree work."

Mitch's eyebrows hitched up—hell, the trainer almost looked disappointed in him being friendly—but he shook with Kyler nonetheless. "No, uh...that's fine." He tilted his head. "Kyler Tate, you say? Why does that ring a bell?"

"I don't know. Maybe it'll come to you."

The trainer scrutinized him another few seconds before shrugging. "Well, let's get out of the rain, shall we?"

Kyler gave Mitch what he hoped was a winning smile. "Great idea. Thanks."

When the other man turned for the barn—shoulders slumped a good deal more than before—Kyler found a mixture of suspicion and amusement on Bree's pretty face. "You see something interesting over here, supergirl?"

"When exactly am I going to get a handle on you?"

He checked the urge to throw an arm around Bree's shoulders, draw her up against his side. "Guess we'll have to wait and see."

They stopped at the entrance to one of the stalls. Inside, a brown horse with patches of white lay down, muscles tense. If Kyler didn't see it with his own eyes, he wouldn't have believed that the mare sighed in relief when it spotted Bree. She murmured something to the animal but made no move to approach, seeming to communicate from ten feet away.

"Her name is Flo-Rida."

He smiled "Like the rapper?"

"Yeah." She leaned into him and pointed at the horse's behind. "But also because she has a white patch in the shape of Florida. The owner's teenage son named her."

"Give that kid a medal."

Mitch cleared his throat behind them, reminding Kyler they weren't alone.

"Looks like you have everything under control for now," Mitch said. "I'm heading out for a bit. Call my number if you need anything."

Ignoring Kyler's grumble over her speaking with another man on the phone, Bree turned to Mitch and nodded. "Will do. Thank you."

If Kyler wasn't mistaken, Mitch looked a little dejected over not being asked to stay, so Kyler took some pity on him. "Wait up, Mitch." He jogged over and met the trainer at the barn entrance. "You mentioned my name ringing a bell. If that's on account of me playing football for Cincinnati and—"

Mitch snapped his fingers. "That's it. Hol-ee shit." He smacked a hand against his outer thigh. "You're playing for the Rage next season."

"Right." Kyler winked over at a dumbstruck Bree, who was probably going nuts not being able to hear their conversation. "I have a line on Bearcats tickets if you're ever up for a drive."

A few minutes later, Kyler's number was programmed into the trainer's phone and Kyler had to admit, not succumbing to jealousy had been harder than evading a tackle, but twice as satisfying.

Returning to Bree at the stall entrance, he leaned down to talk beside her ear. "Aren't you going to go in?"

She turned sparkling, excited eyes on him. "Not unless I'm needed." The backs of their hands brushed together and Kyler's belly tightened up like a drum. Not only because her touch never failed to have an effect, but her love for the animal, for her job, was contagious. "Foals are born naturally. They're cleaned by their mothers afterward and the bonding process begins. I try to stay out of it, only helping if there's a complication."

"Does that happen a lot?" Kyler asked, just to keep her talking in that rushing, euphoric way.

"I wouldn't say a lot. But nature needs a push once in a while." Her excited smile stopped his breath. "That's where I come in."

You want to take her away from this?

Ten gallons of cement coated Kyler's shoulders, hardening immediately. Bree was watching him closely, though, so he forced a casual demeanor. "You were right. The horse does trust you. I could see it." A million thoughts raced in his head, but one stood out brighter than all others. "Dammit, Bree. I'm so proud of you."

"I'm proud of you, too," she whispered, her brows drawing

together at whatever she read on his face. "Kyler?"

Who was he kidding? He'd never been able to hide anything for long from Bree. A fact he'd completely forgotten in the face of seeing how much she thrived in this environment. An environment that might as well be a million miles from Los Angeles.

She started to speak again, but the mare made a distressed sound and stood on shaky legs, sending Bree rushing into the stall.

Chapter Thirteen

Bree's hands were steady, but her adrenaline pumped hot.

Above her, the mare made a long, guttural sound of distress. "Only one of the foal's feet is showing," she explained to Kyler, her voice thick. "We need to stand Flo-Rida up and walk her around. That should hopefully reposition the foal. If it doesn't, I'll have to do it myself."

Without missing a beat, Kyler rubbed his hands together. "Okay. Stand her up and walk around. Let's do this, supergirl."

I'm still in love with him.

Freaking obviously.

Who *wouldn't* love this man? Especially—*God*—when he loved her with so much conviction and patience and persistence. After four years of no communication. He'd signed a multimillion-dollar contract to play professional football. Fame, idolization, and freedom were at his disposal. Yet here was Kyler Tate, same exact man he'd always been—with the addition of some extra drool-worthy muscles—ready to help her deliver a foal on a rainy day in a barn. No questions asked. Because it was what she needed.

It was time, however, that she stopped denying what she needed *most*. That she'd never *stopped* needing. Kyler.

Lord knew she was a stubborn woman and always had been. Kyler was her equal in that way. They'd both spent their separation operating in unique ways. Kyler had bided his time while Bree lived in denial. Had she really believed that someday she would magically get over Kyler? What a farce. Until she took her final breath on this earth, his face would be the first she pictured when someone uttered the word love in her presence. He was her first love and down in the pit of her soul, she'd known he would be her last.

Tucking away the truth for later, Bree blew out a deep breath and stood. After unhooking the bridle from where it hung on the wall, she took care sliding it over the agitated mare's head, whispering comfort to her as she cinched and secured it. With some urging, she led Flo-Rida toward the stall exit, Kyler holding the mare steady on the other side.

"My dad used to be in charge during foaling time. Without him here, the waiting still makes me anxious," Bree murmured. "Talk to me about something."

"I'm going to hook Mitch up with Bearcats tickets," Kyler answered immediately, *shhing* the horse when she made a low whinny. "Despite his name being Mitch."

A chuckle burst free of Bree's lips. "What's wrong with the name Mitch?"

"Nothing. It's perfect. It's exactly what I would name the man I had to battle for your favor."

"But you didn't battle him," she pointed out.

He winked at her over the top of the mare's head. "Didn't I?"

Right there, less than three feet away, was the only person in the world who always managed to make her laugh, grow exasperated, and be surprised, all at the same time. "Where are you going to live in Los Angeles?"

The question slipped out without warning, but Kyler showed no reaction apart from his grip creaking on the reins. "They put us in a hotel for training camp. It gives us time to find a place to call home." He slid her a glance. "I don't know what this life is going to bring, Bree. I could be traded after a few years. Find myself down in Dallas or up in New York. So I figured while...we're in California, we should live by the ocean. Someplace small that makes the change not seem so huge. Two bedrooms, a giant bathtub. A big, floppy dog sleeping on the end of our bed."

A wrench fell in her stomach. "Low blow."

His mouth ticked up at the corner, hope flaring in his green eyes. "I've had some nervous energy on my hands over the last couple days waiting for you to have a good think, so I've been looking at apartments." A beat passed. "I don't know if you still have the same plans, supergirl, but if you wanted to attend a four-year veterinary school, Western University is only a short drive away."

"My plans haven't changed." The wings of fear and excitement tickled her throat, battling one another. "You looked into all that for me?"

"Made sure there was a diner within walking distance of the apartment, too. I know that's how you like to get your coffee."

Her knees wobbled. "Never really got into Starbucks."

"I know."

"Something so formal about ordering coffee off a menu," she whispered under her breath, just to fill the charged silence. "Whipped cream on coffee doesn't seem like it should be an everyday thing."

They reached the wall of the barn and gently turned the mare around, Bree running a hand down her flank. "In the off-season, we could come back to Bloomfield," Kyler continued, his tone low, bordering on urgent. "Whatever you want."

"What about what you want?"

"I want *us*," he rasped. "I'll build everything else around that. That has been my plan since age thirteen. It just got delayed."

"Kyler. This is crazy." The slow pace of their walk was a stark contrast to Bree's rapid heartbeat. The gravity that continued to consume and release her, wrecking her balance. "Can we really ever come back, though? All the attention that follows you around..." She shook her head. "Before college, it was town pride. Now it's curiosity and people standing outside the gym or crowding you to death in Nelson's—"

"I'll keep it away from you." Threads of determination stitched themselves together in Kyler's voice. "No more dragging you out into the open, Bree. I've learned my lesson."

"You can't stop being yourself, Ky. I wouldn't want you to stop."

"Where does that leave me?" he whispered to himself.

Bree ached to take a leap, but impulsive decisions were never how she'd worked. Time and pro/con lists, testing the waters. That's how she operated. Once upon a time, Kyler had been her listening ear. Her sounding board. So while she wanted desperately to leap into his arms, kiss his mouth, and agree to California, she wasn't quite ready. Not without laying some things to rest in her mind.

They reached the stall and Bree guided Flo-Rida back down onto the pallet, observing for long minutes while the mare labored. When she saw both legs emerge, confirming the foal had been repositioned during their walk, Bree fell back on her butt with a sigh of relief, remaining there under the false assumption her heart rate would slow now that the danger had passed. But it didn't.

"Talk to me," Kyler said, threading his fingers through her curls. "Tell me what's holding you back. Tell me what you didn't say on prom night."

"My family needs me," she breathed. "I belong here. In Bloomfield."

"There's more."

Bree looked up to find Kyler watching her from beneath hooded eyelids, seeing straight through to her center. "I've never stopped aching over hurting you. It was the worst night of my life."

"Mine, too." Mouth in a grim line, Kyler scooped Bree up and carried her from the stall. "Talk to me."

She shoved his shoulder, but he didn't budge. "I'm getting there."

Just outside the stall, he set her down, backing her up against the wooden partition. Intensity radiated from every inch of his rock-wall body. "I'll just wait here and be patient. Sound good?"

A laugh shuddered out of her, but it held little humor. Spiked wheels turned in her belly, digging in and getting stuck. "My mother left when we needed her." Words she'd never said out loud poured free, through the cracks of a smashed dam. "She wanted more. I'm afraid to admit I want more, too. Even to myself."

The tension lines around Kyler's mouth softened. "It isn't more, Bree. It's *different*."

"It's *more*. It's California, money and fame and all the things *she* wanted. I'm betraying my family by accepting them, by wanting them, aren't I?"

"I could tell you no, but you're the one who has to believe it."

"That's annoyingly logical." She dropped her forehead onto his chest. "My father would never say it out loud, but I know he feels like a failure for not making her happy. I can't be his instant replay."

Kyler sighed hard, pressing kisses into her hair. "He gave you *this*. Being a vet. As much as I'll bust my ass to make you happy, this will always be something that's yours. And his. You'll never stop sharing it with him, no matter where you are. Los Angeles or Bloomfield."

"It won't be the same." She looked around the barn and thought of her clients. The animals. Familiar faces. Her routine. And the ground shook beneath her at the thought of leaving it all behind. But the idea of Kyler going to Los Angeles without her? It wasn't just tremors beneath her feet. It was a ten on the seismograph. "I can't—"

From the stall came a long, guttural sound, following by the rustling of the ground, the pallet stuffing. Bree and Kyler moved to the opening of the stall, peeking around the edge to find a newborn foal being licked by his mother, tail to head. No matter how many times she witnessed the miracles of her profession, these moments never failed to amaze her. She cupped a hand around her mouth, laughing into it with pure joy.

But when she turned to Kyler to capture his reaction, to store it away in her heart, he was watching her instead. And for once, she couldn't read his expression.

Chapter Fourteen

What if the best way to make Bree happy…was to leave her?

Walk away from her, remembering this moment of total rapture on her face? And just admitting that he'd failed, so that she could succeed.

There were so many snapshots in his memory of Bree as a girl, smiling up at him, just like this, usually when they were alone and he did something goofy. Or when they'd reached the very top of that Ferris wheel, that misty fall morning a million years ago, sunlight breaking through the clouds to kiss her face.

"Ky?"

This wasn't Bree the girl, though. Now she was a woman and she'd found a way to make herself happy, all by herself. She was the same Bree, with new, amazing differences. Changes she'd carved into her heart, without him there to witness it.

When she said his name again, it was a short punctuation, her mouth snapping shut afterward. "Ky."

She reached up with both hands, smoothing fingers over his eyebrows, looking almost frustrated as she searched his face. That was a first. He'd never been capable of mystifying her, nor had he ever tried. He cleared his throat, determined to reassure her, but he stopped himself. What would he say? His world seemed determined to break apart and the only thing keeping it together was Bree's touch exploring his features, tracing down the grooves of his cheeks, sliding up into his hair.

More. Whatever would happen tomorrow, he needed more of Bree now. Needed to hold on tight while time seemed to rush around them, unable to be controlled.

"Say something," she whispered. And it was the fear in her eyes that compelled him forward. The need to rid her of it.

"Everything is going to be fine," he murmured, grasping her wrists, holding her warm palms against his face. "I understand now, Bree."

"Y-you understand—"

His mouth stopped Bree's question, his tongue savoring her jagged gasp. Color exploded in his mind, splattering on the backs of his eyelids in patterns. God, the taste of her was a fucking work of art. Her gasp, the way she tilted her tits up. None of it could be helped. Just the music they made together.

There was some reservation in her kiss, the stroke of her tongue hesitant against the insistence of his. So Kyler used his grip on her curls to tilt her head, branding her mouth with hot slants of lips and hunger, reminding her nothing took precedence over the need they shared. It was alive, sliding warm and liquid down from their belly buttons. Preparing them. His head might be on fire with regret and worry, but nothing burned hotter than they did. It was the definite he needed right now.

Bree caved to his urgency, tension leaving her neck, making it fall to one side. Kyler took advantage of the opening, racing his open lips up the smooth column, clamping the lobe of her ear between his teeth. At the very same time, he fit his erection into the notch of her thighs, ramming her lower body against the partition. "Where?"

"Where?" Bree gasped. "Where what?"

"Focus." Those legs snapped around his hips like they'd been painted on, tearing a groan from his throat. "Where in this barn can I fill up the pussy I was born to satisfy? Give me an answer, supergirl. Going to take off my jeans and wear you instead."

Rain pounded on the barn's roof. Thunder rolled. Lightning struck and lit up the space with white light. Or maybe it was all taking place in her eyes. Kyler couldn't tell. Only knew if he didn't bury himself inside his woman, if he didn't plead for pleasure from her body with his own, he might not survive to the next minute. "H'um...there?" She jerked a thumb over her shoulder at nowhere in particular, never taking her gaze off his mouth. "Thereabouts."

Kyler's laugh was rife with pain and starvation, but he marched in the direction she'd indicated, entering the first empty stall and pinning her sexy, giving body up against the far wall. They were covered by darkness, except for the occasional burst of lightning, making Kyler's groping hands seem like an act of nature. Hell, they were. His God-given humanity was in total control now, feeding on his woman. As though her kisses, the welcome of her body, could sustain him until the world ceased.

"Need to get your shorts and panties off," he muttered huskily, cupping his hands beneath her knees. Raising them and grinding down against her center until she cried out. "Can't let you unwrap these sick legs just yet, though. Ride my dick, Bree. Break me. Tease me. Give me an excuse to be rough."

Her position didn't give her much room to move, but Christ almighty, she worked with what she had. Reaching between their heaving bodies, she lifted the hem of her T-shirt, displaying her silk-cupped tits. Then her hips started circling in a rhythm designed to kill a man. Her fingernails sunk into his shoulders through the material of his shirt, her pussy dragging over his pulsing inches in a torturous dance that left Kyler sucking in deep gulps of breath. Running the tip of his tongue over the hills of her cleavage, leaving a trail in his wake, Kyler took her ass in both hands, moving her in the pattern she'd started, shattering his control one grind at a time.

But when she blinked those bedroom eyes up at him and flexed her thighs, whispering, "There's your excuse," Kyler lost his grip on reality.

Growling low in his throat, he shoved her legs down, tearing aside the cups of her bra with bared teeth. With one of her nipples sucked into his mouth, he unzipped her shorts and wrenched them down, along with her panties, grunting an unspoken command to kick them off. As soon as she was bare from the waist down, Bree dropped her right hand from his shoulder and freed his cock in a few frantic movements.

"Now, now, now, Ky. Please."

His middle finger slipped through her folds, finding her dripping wet, and his dick jerked up against his abdomen, making his teeth clench on a moan. Insistent hunger clawed at the walls of his stomach, weighing down his balls like hot, liquid metal. Taking his hurting inches in one hand, he positioned himself against Bree's tight entrance and filled her in one bone-rattling thrust. His mouth clamped over hers just in time to catch her scream of his name, and he swallowed it, savoring the way it vibrated on the way down.

"Just once I'd love to be between these thighs in a fucking bed, Bree. You have any idea what I would give for that?" He pulled out and drove deep, consuming another one of her screams, reveling in the pain of her nails breaking skin through his T-shirt. "My fucking soul. I would hand it right over."

"Oh my God." Her eyes were blind, words pushed out from between her teeth, her thighs tight and trembling around his waist. "Doesn't matter where. Feels so good. Kyler, *don't stop.*"

"It *matters.*" He ground their foreheads together, beginning to pump in earnest, one forceful drive after the other. "Where I fuck the love of my life matters. I want to buy sheets together, bring them home, and lick you until they're drenched. I don't want time limits or worrying if we'll get caught. I'm a goddamn man and I want my woman beside me when I sleep, Bree."

"I picture you beside me sometimes." The treasure blew out of her in a rush and unglued him, deconstructed him into tiny pieces. He could only absorb the impact as she planted kisses on his face, rubbing circles onto his chest with the heels of her hands, down his back. "When I'm nervous or I have a big surgery the next day, I think of you lying beside me, telling me it'll be all right. That afterward, it'll just be you and me."

"Bree," he croaked, pressure pushing inward on his skull. "Fuck, Bree. I almost died from missing you."

"I'm sorry. I'm *sorry.*"

There it was. Those two words were the answer he'd come to Bloomfield afraid to hear, weren't they? She couldn't come with him. Taking her to Los Angeles would dim the beautiful glow inside her, and he wouldn't be responsible for that. No way in hell. Kyler wouldn't fault her for it, though. Being angry at Bree never lasted because the love smashed it. Always would.

The call of his body to give her satisfaction rose to a fever pitch, moving his hips in greedy drives. Jesus, he'd always been twice Bree's size, but he'd grown broader, more solid, and she bounced off the hard surface of his body now with loud, moist slaps, her legs spread for his cock. She tossed her head back and gave hot, little whimpers every time her tits jiggled with the force of his thrusts. And Lord help him, he adored every gorgeous inch of her. Knowing her glow came from the inside made her twice as beautiful. His open mouth planted itself over hers, stealing her exhales and filling his lungs with them. "You'll always be mine, won't you?"

"Same as you'll always be mine."

Tongue twining with hers, he used his grip on her ass to hold her steady for a final series of drives, committing the increased shaking of her thighs to memory. The way she sucked in a gasp and held it, her brown eyes darkening, chin dropping. His cock throbbed, on the verge of release, but he held fast and waited, waited, for her to go hurtling past the finish line, her head falling back and slamming against the wall, muscles tensing and shuddering. "Oh…my God. *Kyler.*"

"Bree. *I love you.* My girl. *Always* mine."

He kissed her though the end of her storm and the beginning of his.

And when it was over, everything in his world had been rearranged.

Chapter Fifteen

"You can't be here. How did you get this address?" Raised male voices cut through the lethargic haze of Bree's mind. She sat up and looked around at the darkened interior of the truck, moonlight spilling across the dashboard. Eleven-thirty said the clock. No wonder she was exhausted. After two restless nights, the foal's birth, and Kyler taking her in the barn, fatigue had hit her like a two-by-four. The last thing she remembered was Kyler snagging the keys and telling her to catch some z's. "This is my girlfriend's house. She—you need to leave. Now, please."

Bree forced her heavy eyelids to widen and found Kyler outside the truck. He continued to shift left and right, blocking her view of the man he argued with. Argued with…in her driveway?

Her fingers went to the door handle, curling around it, but she recoiled when a bright light cut through the night and blinded her. The man held a camera.

"Training camp starts next week and the Rage has been chosen for a documentary. This is just preliminary stuff," said the stranger. "Couldn't hunt you down at your parents' house and someone in town was kind enough to direct me here. Your girlfriend, you say?"

Again, the light crept over Kyler's shoulder, so intrusive and stark. Bree covered her face and scooted toward the driver's side, climbing out, but remaining hidden behind the truck. "Ky?"

"Bree, go on inside. It's going to be all right." Kyler spoke without turning to look at her. His back and shoulder muscles strained beneath his white T-shirt, hands balled in fists, his posture daring the man to raise his camera one more time. Her suspicion was confirmed a moment later when he gritted out, "Lift that camera and you'll never find all the pieces."

A low whistle came from the stranger. "I get it, man. You're protective. Must be serious, then. How long have you been dating? How do you think she'll manage while you're on the road? Any plans for a family?"

"*Bree.*"

Surprisingly, her instinct wasn't to run. The spotlight usually sent her tearing off to the closest parking lot. But fleeing didn't even occur to her in that moment. No, leaving Kyler to handle the situation alone felt wrong. Her instinct demanded she go to him, pull him inside. Let the jerk cameraman take whatever pictures he wanted. They weren't doing anything wrong. They were two people who loved one another. Why should they hide themselves away?

How would she handle Kyler going on the road? They'd survived *four years*. Mere days would be child's play. She almost had the urge to laugh.

There was nothing funny about Kyler's demeanor, though. And she was far too fatigued to fight this battle tonight. They didn't *need* to fight any battle but their own, and tomorrow would be soon enough. Los Angeles was light years away and she still needed to examine the move from every angle. Kyler would understand. He would be patient, as always. They would figure out what came next in their life together when she could keep her eyes open.

"Come inside," she called. "Come with me."

Finally he turned, a wealth of turbulence in his eyes. So much undisguised emotion, her stomach began to churn. "I'll handle this. You go in."

She shook her head. "No."

"Please, Bree. This is your home." Then quieter, "I did this."

"If you're not gone in thirty seconds, I'm calling the police." Bree lifted her chin and made a little shooing motion toward the cameraman. "I'm counting."

Kyler stood there with his back turned to her long after the red sedan disappeared down the driveway. With exhaustion weighing heavy on her shoulders, both of them locked inside the darkness, she felt as if she were in a dream. Nothing seemed real. Not the cameraman, not the new, shimmering image in her mind of a home on the beach, a floppy dog on the bed. Definitely not the new confidence and strength in her bones, possibly ready to embrace change. None of it.

"Kyler," she whispered, going up behind him, laying kisses along the breadth of his shoulders. "Tuck me in?"

Turning, he made a gruff noise and led her inside by the hand. Her father had left the front door unlocked, but after what happened, she reasoned they should be cautious. Kyler watched as she turned the bolt with a pained expression, obviously still upset over the scene in the driveway. "Hey, I don't think he'll be back." She tugged him down the hallway toward her bedroom, keeping her voice to a whisper. "Once he discovers the cast of characters in Bloomfield, he won't need a sound bite from me. They'll keep him entertained."

Bree didn't bother turning on the light in her bedroom. She simply kicked off her shoes, dropped her jean shorts, and curled into a fetal position on the bed. It wasn't until sleep started to descend like a heavy metal curtain did she realize Kyler still stood just inside the door, silent and still as a statue.

"Where's my kiss?" Bree murmured, turning onto her back.

He moved so fast, she'd barely managed to suck in a breath before Kyler planted his hands on the mattress, caging her in...and delivered a knock-out blow courtesy of his mouth. There was something about the kiss that snagged her memory, but she was too consumed to place it. Her limbs turned to jelly, her fingers grappling with the bedspread. The insides of her thighs began to itch, greedy for his hips to settle between them, but he broke contact before it could happen.

"Sleep, supergirl," he said huskily, planting his lips on her forehead. "Everything will look better in the morning."

A tingle on the back of Bree's neck commanded her to go after him, but it took too long for her legs to move. His tall, reliable form disappeared through the doorway, the outline of him lingering and renewing the notion she was dreaming. And then there was nothing.

* * * *

Bree woke up smiling. She'd had the *best* dream. One she'd had many times in the past, but not recently. Not since Kyler left. And now she knew why.

She was supposed to be with him. Wherever he went.

Sitting up in bed, her heart was bursting with certainty from the remnants of her dream. Kyler standing on a green lawn, sunlight catching on the stubble adorning his chin and cheeks. Behind him, a house, modest and loved. A flannel shirt was tucked crookedly into the waistband of Kyler's jeans because he'd been wrestling with their two boys and a big, clumsy dog. Footballs, dog toys, and bikes laying haphazardly every few feet on the grass.

This image, one she'd had a thousand times, had never been more vivid. Never more real. She could smell the chimney smoke in the air, feel the love in Kyler's eyes as they reached her across the yard.

Bree gasped out loud at the impact of it. She needed to go see him now. Spending even one night apart seemed ridiculous all of a sudden. Or maybe it always had. She didn't know. Didn't know, but they would sort through everything together as soon as they were in the same room. Being away from him was causing this horrible ache. One that made her hands flutter over the spot, a lump sticking in her throat.

When her gaze landed on the bedside clock, Bree knew why. It was past one o'clock in the afternoon. Kyler's flight left for Los Angeles today.

Bree's blood chilled as memories from last night began to trickle in. The cameraman in the driveway. *I did this*, Kyler had said. Then…then that kiss. The familiarity of it.

Because he'd only ever given her a kiss like that once before. To say good-bye when she ended things on prom night.

"No. No. He wouldn't leave yet." Bree's feet twisted in the sheet on the way out of bed, almost knocking her to the floor. In a daze, she went to the bathroom and brushed her teeth, not seeing herself in the mirror. Seeing nothing except Kyler's unreadable expression last night in the barn.

Everything is going to be fine. I understand now.

He understood what? Why…why she couldn't go with him? Why she needed to stay? That's what they'd been talking about, right? Los Angeles. Bree's mother. All the cons on the list of why Bree couldn't go with him. But none of the pros.

None of the reasons why she *could.*

Her bloodless fingers dropped the toothbrush in the sink, fear slicing straight up her middle.

He'd left.

Last night, he'd been saying good-bye.

Cymbals crashed in Bree's head, balance deserting her as she ran back into her bedroom. Blood beat in her temples, her lungs scraped raw from dragging in jagged breaths. She pulled on the jean shorts still resting on the floor, shoved her feet into galoshes, and ran for the house's front door. Rainclouds covered the sun, shrouding the house in gloom, moisture pouring down the windows.

She turned in a circle, trying to gather her bearings, but it didn't work. Various images of Kyler cycled one by one through her consciousness. Dancing. Speaking to her outside the diner, casual ease forced into his voice. How could she have missed his determination? Had she been blind? Kyler across from her at the dinner table, driving beside her, walking the mare.

"Oh, please." Bree grabbed her stomach and jogged toward the door. "Oh God, please."

If he'd already left, changing Kyler's mind would be a feat equivalent to turning back time. Convincing him she wanted—*needed*—to come along would be impossible if she let the deadline of his flight pass. The man did what he thought was best for her. Never failed. And she'd stupidly given him every reason to leave, to set her free.

I don't want to be free of him. Being free of Kyler is the real prison.

Just before Bree reached the door, something stopped her in her tracks. The family portrait—which included her mother—that had been hanging since she was a child…had been replaced. The new photograph featured her father, her sister, and herself. Just the three of them.

It was the look in her own eye that captured Bree's attention. It wasn't far off and disconnected, the way her mother's had been. No. She was present, looking down at Kira lovingly, her hand resting over Samuel's where it lay on her shoulder.

A light went on behind her. "You could be a million miles away and we'd still feel you here. With us." Her father's voice came from the dining room, strong and steady. Full of affection. "You're not abandoning us, Bree. You never could."

She pressed the back of her hand over her mouth for a beat. "I abandoned him, though, didn't I? Now I'm too late."

"You're underestimating him." Her father's long-suffering sigh turned Bree around. "I wouldn't say that unless I meant it."

"I know." She pointed an accusing finger at her father but didn't have the strength to keep her arm up. "You love him, too."

"Don't push it." With a wink, he jerked his head toward the door. "Go."

Bree rushed out into the rain without an umbrella, going straight for her truck. She pulled down the sun visor and the keys dropped into her lap, where Kyler had apparently left them. Such a simple gesture, but it made a sob rise in Bree's throat as she gunned the truck in reverse down the driveway. Before turning onto the street, she caught sight of a red sedan parked on the main road. In the driver's seat, a man watched her with a cautious smile.

An idea formed. But it would only work if Kyler hadn't left.

And an awful pit in her stomach yawned wide, telling her...he had.

* * * *

Bree's worst fear was confirmed when she pulled up in front of Kyler's home.

There wasn't a vehicle in sight.

Not his truck, not his daddy's. His mother's station wagon was gone, too.

Were they seeing him off at the airport? Was Kyler already on the way home, his plane nothing but a speck in the air on its way to Los Angeles?

She climbed out of the truck on shaky legs, her galoshes sinking into the mud, making her slip forward. The red sedan pulled up behind her in the driveway, the cameraman stepping out with plastic already positioned over his head and the camera. A look of sympathy skittered across his face before he hid it.

God, she could very well have brought this man along to witness her humiliation. She was too late. Had to be. Why would Kyler wait around for someone who'd doubted what they had together? Over and over. She wouldn't even blame him if he'd given up and left.

Rain coasted down Bree's cheeks as she walked slowly for the front door. Each footstep sank into the mud, as though God was trying to inform her this was a fool's mission. The cameraman's footsteps echoed hers, *glopping* every couple seconds in the mud. A slow-moving funeral procession.

Finally, she'd climbed the steps and stood outside the door. Her knock sounded so hollow, ringing back at her from inside the empty house. The rain began falling heavier, pounding the ground around the Tate house, thunder rolling far off in the distance.

Still, she knocked again, harder. "Kyler?"

The camera light went on behind her, reflecting in the brass doorknob, but Bree no longer cared about having an audience for her worst moment. No, there had always been far more at stake with Kyler than stupid cameras could ever capture. She would welcome hundreds of them in her face as long as Kyler held her at the end of the day, issuing challenges in her ear. Calling her—

"Supergirl?"

For a second, Bree thought it was her imagination conjuring Kyler's voice. She whipped around toward the cameraman, but he was no longer pointing his device at her. No, the light shined on Kyler where he stood at the base of the steps, rain pouring down his head, dripping off his chin.

He was the most incredible, most beautiful sight she'd ever seen. Relief caught her so hard in the belly, she slumped back against the door, pinned there by the miracle she'd been given.

Kyler shot up the steps, concern etched on his beloved face. "Bree? What's wrong?" He turned wild eyes on the cameraman, who wisely backed up but kept filming. "Don't worry, I'm going to take care of this. It won't happen again—"

"No. No, he's... I asked him to come." Her hands trembled as she swiped at the rain in her face. "Oh God, I-I thought you'd left. I thought you'd *left*."

Bree didn't realize she'd slid down the door into a sitting position until Kyler went to his knees, crawling toward her. "Hey." He cupped her face in two warm hands, his green eyes blazing. "I told you, Bree. I said it and you heard me. I'm not leaving without you."

"But your flight—"

"I missed it." His gaze moved over her face, catching on her eyelids, stray curls, her nose, mouth. "Your home is here. This is where you're happy—"

"No, wait—"

"So I'm staying." He shook her and repeated himself. "I'm staying. That's how this was always going to work if you didn't decide to come, supergirl. You just weren't hearing me all the way."

For the next few moments, the sound of rain falling and her tortured heartbeat was all she could hear. "You were going to give it up for me?"

"Not were. Am." His thumbs skated over her lips. "None of it means a damn thing without you, Bree. I'm getting a little tired of saying it and not having you believe me."

"So stop." Lord, she couldn't get her breath. This man. He was one and the same with her dreams. "Stop saying it. Because it means something to me." She desperately tried to gather her thoughts. "I dreamed of you last night. Sons. We had sons. A yard and a dog. And you loved me. I could feel how much you loved me, clear across the yard." Her voice fell to a whisper. "Clear from Cincinnati."

Kyler's eyes turned glassy, his breath escaping in a giant rush. "Damn right I love you."

"California is the first step in that journey. We're going to take it together. I *want* to, Kyler. I don't want to stay here and wonder what we could have seen and done. Our *own* life. All the things that'll steer it. The directions we'll take." Tears mixed with rain on her cheeks. "I want to go with you."

He stayed very still, but hope livened his features. "Do you mean that?"

Bree was still nodding when he launched himself at her, wrapping her in a bear hug and hauling her onto his lap. They fell back onto the porch in the glow of the camera, still wrapped up in each other's arms. "Christ. I thought I was imagining you standing on this porch, Bree."

She clung to his neck. "Where were you?"

"Walking through the cornfields. Deciding on my next move with you."

Her heart tripled its tempo. "What did you come up with?"

"I got as far as another dance off…" They both stopped to laugh, Kyler rubbing their noses together. "But I decided to go for broke and propose instead." His hand went to his pocket, coming back with a simple antique engagement ring between two fingers. His expression turned serious, even in the wake of Bree's gulping cry of his name. "I was going to refuse to take no for an answer. In case you're wondering, that part hasn't changed."

"Ask me," Bree murmured, framing his face with her hands.

"Be my wife, supergirl. Let me love you from across the yard."

"Yes."

A slow clap started from the base of the steps. Clearly having forgotten about their audience, Bree and Kyler both turned to look to find the cameraman flipping off the light and lowering his device. "Congratulations." He turned away and started toward his car. "And good luck next season."

"Who needs luck when I've got Bree Justice?" Kyler blew her mind with a slow, drugging kiss, his mouth hot and uncompromising. "Why did you bring him along?"

"To show you I'm going to be okay. There's just you and me, Ky." She licked into his mouth and moaned when he shifted his hips. "The rest is just noise," she gasped.

"Come for a walk in the cornfields with me."

"In the rain?"

That challenging expression she knew so well made Bree's heart float up, up into the clouds. "Scared?"

"Scared?" She shook her head. "No. I'll go anywhere with you."

Minutes later, they disappeared into the stalks, eternity stretching out around them and in front of them.

Epilogue

Kyler had expected attention and cameras. He hadn't planned on national interest in his and Bree's relationship. Only this time, *she'd* been the one dragging *him* into the spotlight. And boy, did she appear to be reveling in the turnabout.

During their first week in Los Angeles, Kyler and his fiancée had been recognized on the street by well-wishers, media, and Rage fans everywhere they went, thanks to the viral video of his proposal. The first time they'd been approached and asked for a picture, he'd gone tense, but Bree didn't so much as flinch, flashing her beautiful smile at the cameras he'd once dreaded.

Signing the lease on their apartment and enrolling Bree in the veterinary medicine program at Western University was the first order of business, before Kyler fell into the full-throttle hell of training camp. Every morning, Bree sent him off with a sleepy kiss and each night he crawled into bed beside her, pushing textbooks and binders out of the way before pulling her into his arms and passing out.

Yes, they finally had a damn bed. Since they'd forgone putting down expensive roots in California right away, they'd splurged on the most extravagant bed Kyler could find, tricking it out with soft sheets and feather pillows. The only trouble with their first shared bed was getting out of it. And on their mutual days off, they didn't even bother trying, only emerging from the bedroom for food. Or to take a walk on the beach, which stretched out from the end of their block, straight through to forever, a lot like the cornfields they often missed.

Bree's fall semester coincided with football season, so those days were few and far between, but they only treasured them more. No amount of time or difficulty could touch them. Commitment was in the way they looked at one another. Not a damn thing, especially some days apart, could test their bond. It was airtight.

Today was Kyler's first regular season game. Walking out onto the field, a flashback to high school hit him. Bree up in the stands, red-faced over the way everyone stared at her when his name was announced. The ooohs and kissing noises. High school stuff.

This stadium full of thousands of roaring fans? *Not* high school stuff. Truth be told, Kyler lost his ever-loving cool envisioning Bree in the center of it all. Recognizable. Alone, despite the team security that escorted the players' family members. His hands clenched in the leather gloves, his gaze searching uselessly through the writhing crowd for her face.

She's there. You're going home to her. Relax.

Easier said than done.

Taking a deep breath, Kyler prepared to put his helmet back on when a sign caught his eye, just even with the fifty-yard line, about four rows back.

It said, "Supergirl," and had an arrow pointing downward, at the only person who could calm him down in that moment. Bree.

Relief and love rocked him back on his heels. Especially when Bree stood and Kyler saw that she wore his jersey. She blew him a kiss and turned around… And on the back, above his number—instead of Tate—the name read, "Superguy."

Leave it to Bree to make him feel invincible.

And that day, he was. And *every* day, they were.

THE END

* * * *

Also from 1001 Dark Nights and Tessa Bailey, discover Rough Rhythm.

Sign up for the 1001 Dark Nights Newsletter
and be entered to win a Tiffany Key necklace.

There's a contest every month!

Go to www.1001DarkNights.com to subscribe.

As a bonus, all subscribers will receive a free
1001 Dark Nights story
The First Night
by Lexi Blake & M.J. Rose

Discover 1001 Dark Nights Collection Four

Go to www.1001DarkNights.com for more information.

ROCK CHICK REAWAKENING by Kristen Ashley
A Rock Chick Novella

ADORING INK by Carrie Ann Ryan
A Montgomery Ink Novella

SWEET RIVALRY by K. Bromberg

SHADE'S LADY by Joanna Wylde
A Reapers MC Novella

RAZR by Larissa Ione
A Demonica Underworld Novella

ARRANGED by Lexi Blake
A Masters and Mercenaries Novella

TANGLED by Rebecca Zanetti
A Dark Protectors Novella

HOLD ME by J. Kenner
A Stark Ever After Novella

SOMEHOW, SOME WAY by Jennifer Probst
A Billionaire Builders Novella

TOO CLOSE TO CALL by Tessa Bailey
A Romancing the Clarksons Novella

HUNTED by Elisabeth Naughton
An Eternal Guardians Novella

EYES ON YOU by Laura Kaye
A Blasphemy Novella

BLADE by Alexandra Ivy/Laura Wright
A Bayou Heat Novella

DRAGON BURN by Donna Grant
A Dark Kings Novella

TRIPPED OUT by Lorelei James
A Blacktop Cowboys® Novella

STUD FINDER by Lauren Blakely

MIDNIGHT UNLEASHED by Lara Adrian
A Midnight Breed Novella

HALLOW BE THE HAUNT by Heather Graham
A Krewe of Hunters Novella

DIRTY FILTHY FIX by Laurelin Paige
A Fixed Novella

THE BED MATE by Kendall Ryan
A Room Mate Novella

NIGHT GAMES by CD Reiss
A Games Novella

NO RESERVATIONS by Kristen Proby
A Fusion Novella

DAWN OF SURRENDER by Liliana Hart
A MacKenzie Family Novella

Discover 1001 Dark Nights Collection One

Go to www.1001DarkNights.com for more information.

FOREVER WICKED by Shayla Black
CRIMSON TWILIGHT by Heather Graham
CAPTURED IN SURRENDER by Liliana Hart
SILENT BITE: A SCANGUARDS WEDDING by Tina Folsom
DUNGEON GAMES by Lexi Blake
AZAGOTH by Larissa Ione
NEED YOU NOW by Lisa Renee Jones
SHOW ME, BABY by Cherise Sinclair
ROPED IN by Lorelei James
TEMPTED BY MIDNIGHT by Lara Adrian
THE FLAME by Christopher Rice
CARESS OF DARKNESS by Julie Kenner

Also from 1001 Dark Nights

TAME ME by J. Kenner

Discover 1001 Dark Nights Collection Two

Go to www.1001DarkNights.com for more information.

WICKED WOLF by Carrie Ann Ryan
WHEN IRISH EYES ARE HAUNTING by Heather Graham
EASY WITH YOU by Kristen Proby
MASTER OF FREEDOM by Cherise Sinclair
CARESS OF PLEASURE by Julie Kenner
ADORED by Lexi Blake
HADES by Larissa Ione
RAVAGED by Elisabeth Naughton
DREAM OF YOU by Jennifer L. Armentrout
STRIPPED DOWN by Lorelei James
RAGE/KILLIAN by Alexandra Ivy/Laura Wright
DRAGON KING by Donna Grant
PURE WICKED by Shayla Black
HARD AS STEEL by Laura Kaye
STROKE OF MIDNIGHT by Lara Adrian
ALL HALLOWS EVE by Heather Graham
KISS THE FLAME by Christopher Rice
DARING HER LOVE by Melissa Foster
TEASED by Rebecca Zanetti
THE PROMISE OF SURRENDER by Liliana Hart

Also from 1001 Dark Nights

THE SURRENDER GATE By Christopher Rice
SERVICING THE TARGET By Cherise Sinclair

Discover 1001 Dark Nights Collection Three

Go to www.1001DarkNights.com for more information.

About Tessa Bailey

Tessa Bailey is originally from Carlsbad, California. The day after high school graduation, she packed her yearbook, ripped jeans and laptop, driving cross-country to New York City in under four days. Her most valuable life experiences were learned thereafter while waitressing at K-Dees, a Manhattan pub owned by her uncle. Inside those four walls, she met her husband, best friend and discovered the magic of classic rock, managing to put herself through Kingsborough Community College and the English program at Pace University at the same time. Several stunted attempts to enter the work force as a journalist followed, but romance writing continued to demand her attention. She now lives in Long Island, New York with her husband of ten years and five-year-old daughter. Although she is severely sleep-deprived, she is incredibly happy to be living her dream of writing about people falling in love.

Discover More Tessa Bailey

ROUGH RHYTHM
By Tessa Bailey

God help the woman I take home tonight.

Band manager James Brandon never expected to find the elusive satisfaction he'd been chasing, let alone stumble upon it in some sleezy Hollywood meat market. Yet the girl's quiet pride spoke to him from across the bar, louder than a shout. Troubled, hungry and homeless, she'd placed her trust in him. But after losing the grip on his dark desires that one fateful night, James has spent the last four years atoning for letting her down.

This time I'll finally crack him.

Rock band drummer Lita Regina has had enough of James's guilt. She wants the explosive man she met that night in Hollywood. The man who held nothing back and took no prisoners—save Lita. And she'll stop at nothing to revive him. Even if it means throwing herself into peril at every turn, just to get a reaction from her stoic manager. But when Lita takes her quest one step too far, James disappears from her life, thinking his absence will keep her safe.

Now it's up to Lita to bring James back…and ignite an inferno of passion in the process.

Reader Advisory: *ROUGH RHYTHM* contains fantasies of nonconsensual sex, acted upon by consenting characters. Readers with sensitivity to portrayals of nonconsensual sex should be advised.

Too Hard to Forget
Romancing the Clarksons, Book 3
by Tessa Bailey
Now Available

This time, *she's* calling the shots.

Peggy Clarkson is returning to her alma mater with one goal in mind: confront Elliott Brooks, the man who ruined her for all others, and remind him of what he's been missing. Even after three years, seeing him again is like a punch in the gut, but Peggy's determined to stick to her plan. Maybe then, once she has the upper hand, she'll finally be able to move on.

In the years since Peggy left Cincinnati, Elliott has kept his focus on football. No distractions and no complications. But when Peggy walks back onto his practice field and into his life, he knows she could unravel everything in his carefully controlled world. Because the girl who was hard to forget is now a woman *impossible* to resist.

* * * *

Peggy couldn't pinpoint what drew her toward the tunnel. The football game was going to start in just fifteen minutes, and she was supposed to be leading the Bearcat cheerleading squad's warm-ups. But just like always, she was aware of his absence. On the field, pacing the sideline, terse instructions being delivered into his headset, while eagle eyes watched the team stretch and prepare. And in the same way she never failed to sense him nearby, his absence was having the opposite effect now. Instead of feeling hot and full, her stomach was cold and empty.

Pompoms in hand, Peggy walked on the balls of her feet down the silent, airless hall leading to the football team's locker room. She had no authorization to be there but couldn't ignore the pull. She'd find him back there. The man who watched her as if she were the Promised Land one moment, hell the next.

Elliott Brooks. Head coach of the Bearcats. Two-time recipient of the Coach of the Year award. Uncompromising hard ass known for demanding perfection not only from his team, but himself. Devout Catholic. They called him the Kingmaker, because so many of his players had gone on to be first round NFL draft picks. That man. The one who visited her bed nightly.

Well. In her dreams, anyway. In real life, they'd never exchanged a single word. Their long, secretive glances were a language all their own, though. When cheerleading and football practices intersected, his burning coal eyes moved over her like a brush fire.

What are you looking at? *His gaze seemed to ask. But in the same glance, she could read the contradicting subtext.* Don't you *dare* look at anyone on this field but me.

Give me one good reason, *she would blink back, cocking a hip.*

And he would. Commanding the field with a whip crack command, stalking the sidelines like a predatory creature, seeing all, commenting only when strictly necessary. Those eyes would sneak back to her, though. Without fail. Their message would read, I'm a man among boys. There's your reason.

Or she'd imagined everything and the telepathic communication was in her head alone. A scary possibility…and one she couldn't bring herself to believe. Was it finally time to find out?

The crowd's excitement followed Peggy down the long tunnel, fading the closer she came to the locker room. That's when she heard the heavy, measured breaths. The forceful clearing of a man's throat.

His *throat.*

Before she could second-guess her sanity, Peggy stepped into the off-limits room, dropping her pompoms and slamming back against the wall under the weight of his attention. It snapped against her skin like an open hand. God, he was gorgeous, even in his sudden fury. Hard bodied, golden from the sun and righteously male, all stubbled and tall and full of might. The muscles of her abdomen squeezed— squeezed—along with her thighs as he stormed over, his words being directed at her for the very first time.

"What the hell do you think you're doing here?"

Don't lose your nerve now. Years. *She'd been watching him for years. Since she'd entered the university as a freshman. Watched his triumphs from afar. And the horrible tragedy, still so recent. So fresh.* "You should be on the field."

Elliott's crack of masculine laughter held no humor. "And you thought it was your job to come get me, cheerleader?"

So condescending. But accompanied by his raking glance down her thighs and belly…she couldn't help but be turned on by it. She loved him addressing her at all. Finally. "Yeah. I did. Everyone else is probably too scared of you."

Dark eyes narrowing, he stepped closer. So close, she almost whimpered, the fantasies having taken such a deep hold, her longing was on a hair-trigger. "Well, you were wrong. It's not your job. So pick up your sparkly bullshit and move out."

"They're called pompoms and I'll leave when I'm good and ready." With an incredulous expression, Elliott started to move away, telling Peggy she needed to work fast. Toward what goal? She'd come with no plan. Had never expected to actually speak to this man in her life. "I've seen you watching me."

He froze, a muscle leaping in his cheek. "You were mistaken."

"No. I wasn't. I'm not." She wet her lips, gaining confidence when his eyes followed the movement and she saw the hunger. The same hunger she'd watched grow, even while he begrudged it, over the course of the last few months. Since the tragedy. "You don't have to feel ashamed about it. Not now."

His fists planted on either side of her head with a bash, shaking the lockers, then his face hovered mere inches away. "What would you know about shame?"

Wetness rushed between Peggy's thighs as his apples and mint scent took hold of her throat like a giant metal hook. "I know the last six months were awful for you. They would be so hard for anyone. But especially you, because you carry everyone on your back. The whole school lives for Saturdays. If you'll win or lose." His brow furrowed, his scrutiny so intense, she wondered how her legs kept from giving out. They must have moved closer without realizing, because the tips of Peggy's breasts grazed Elliott's chest and he groaned. A harsh, guttural sound that might as well have been a symphony, it was so welcome to her ears.

"You..." His throat flexed. "You don't know anything about me, Peggy."

Her pulse went haywire. The wordless communication hadn't been imaginary. Those hard eyes really had been speaking to her. It was the way he said Peggy. As though he'd tested her name on his tongue a million times. "You know my name."

On behalf of 1001 Dark Nights,

Liz Berry and M.J. Rose would like to thank ~

Steve Berry
Doug Scofield
Kim Guidroz
Jillian Stein
InkSlinger PR
Dan Slater
Asha Hossain
Chris Graham
Pamela Jamison
Fedora Chen
Kasi Alexander
Jessica Johns
Dylan Stockton
Richard Blake
BookTrib After Dark
and Simon Lipskar

Made in the USA
Middletown, DE
30 March 2021

36536609R00080